Learning Corporation of America presents

When We First Met

Starring
Amy Linker and Andrew Sabiston

Directed by
PAUL SALTZMAN

Produced by
ROBERT McDONALD
PAUL SALTZMAN

Line Producer
Production Manager
RAY SZEGHO

Associate Producer
1st Assistant Director
JOHN BOARD

Director of Photography
MARK IRWIN c.s.c.

Art Director
SANDRA KYBARTAS

Location Manager
2nd Assistant Director
MICHAEL MACDONALD

Music Composed by
ALEX PAUK
ZINA LOUIE

Story Editor
SONDRA KELLY

Casting
DIANE POLLEY

Screenplay
AXEL DAIMLER &
NORMA FOX MAZER

Executive Producer
ROBERT McDONALD

An HBO® Exclusive Presentation

**Other Scholastic paperbacks
you will enjoy:**

Anna to the Infinite Power
   by Mildred Ames

Dear Lovey Hart, I Am Desperate
   by Ellen Conford

Jock and Jill
   by Robert Lipsyte

Run, Run, as Fast as You Can
   by Mary Pope Osborne

Sarah Bishop
   by Scott O'Dell

Seven Days to a Brand-New Me
   by Ellen Conford

A Smart Kid like You
   by Stella Pevsner

*We Interrupt This Semester for
an Important Bulletin*
   by Ellen Conford

When We First Met

Norma Fox Mazer

SCHOLASTIC INC.
New York Toronto London Auckland Sydney Tokyo

Material on page 112 reprinted by permission of
Abigail Van Buren for her column on Legal Dilemma.

ISBN 0-590-31987-6

12 11 10 9 8 7 6 5 4 3 2 1   8   4 5 6 7 8 9/8
                    Printed in the U.S.A.   01

Jenny! Shut off the TV and go to the market. We need cream.

Why?

Why what?

Why do we need cream, Gail?

I'm baking, what do you THINK? Are you going to shut off that TV or not?

I'm not watching TV, Gail. I'm doing my homework.

Your homework can wait five minutes. Jenny! Are you listening to me? I need heavy cream and—

Cream is fattening.

Oh! What a mean, nasty thing to say. Just because you're a bunch of bones—

I only meant you could use milk instead.

The recipe, CHILD, calls for cream.

Do you have to follow the recipe slavishly?

Do you have to argue about EVERYTHING, Jenny Pennoyer?

I'm not arguing, Gail. I'm just pointing out in a reasonable—

I WISH you'd grow up, I really do! Fifteen, and you're still acting like five. You act more babyish than Ethel! You just don't know what cooperation means, for instance.

If I'm so young and immature, Gail, how can you send me out into the cruel, cruel world alone? It's raining! Aren't I too young to—

Oh, shut up. I'll go.

I didn't say I wouldn't go.

Forget it!

I'll GO, Gail.

I said, FORGET IT!

Gail! Gail, come on . . . come back . . . don't go. . . . Let's do this all over again. I was just teasing you. Gail? Can you hear me? Don't take the bike, Gail. Gail? Gail? Don't, Gail! Don't . . . don't . . . don't. . .

WOMAN CHARGED IN FATAL CRASH

Mrs. Nell Montana, 36, of 45 East Street, pleaded innocent Friday in a city Police Court to charges in connection with a fatal car-bike accident early Sunday evening. Police Court Judge J. Robert Saterino ordered Mrs. Montana held in lieu of $15,000 bail pending a court appearance on a charge of second-degree manslaughter. She is also scheduled to reappear March 25 on counts of driving while intoxicated, speeding, and running a stop sign.

Police said they arrested the suspect after the vehicle she was driving was involved in a collision with a bicycle ridden by Gail Pennoyer, 16, of 2803 Pittmann Street. Miss Pennoyer, who suffered head and internal injuries in the 4:55 P.M. crash on a rain-slick road at Nugent and Elroy Streets, died at about 8 A.M. Tuesday at Upstate Medical Center.

Chapter 1

It was March when Jenny first saw Rob in his rainbow suspenders. March was a month she had never liked—the way it played around with feelings, tantalizing with the thought that winter was over and spring was coming, promising but never delivering. March, to Jenny, was wet, raw days with the wind sharp through her jacket. It was dark gray mornings and greasy rain running down the windows. March was the month when her spirits sank. March was the month her sister Gail had died. And yet March was the month she first saw Rob in his rainbow suspenders.

The moment she walked into the auditorium she noticed the blond boy sitting a little forward of the balcony. His head glinted like a gold coin in the dimness. In that first instant Jenny saw him completely; absorbed him, as it were, into herself. The curly gold head, blue shirt, rainbow suspenders—but these were details. He leaned forward as if about to call out to her. And something happened to Jenny. Stunned, she sat down next to Rhoda.

"Ready?" Rhoda asked.

Jenny slid halfway around in her seat. The golden-haired boy was still leaning forward, intently watching her. Color mounted in her face. *Who is he?* Something winged and strong beat inside her. Was this the unnameable "it" for which she had been waiting so long?

"Want one?" Rhoda offered her a mint Lifesaver.

"Thanks. My favorite." Jenny pulled her braids forward over her shoulders. She was a tall, slender girl with a narrow, high-ridged nose. Years ago, someone had described her as a "Modigliani girl." She had found the Italian's paintings in the library—girls with narrow, lopsided faces and eyes shaped like primitive fish, which stared somberly out into the world—and never since had thought herself pretty.

Rhoda disagreed. "You're striking-looking."

Nice of Rhoda. Remembering helped Jenny not to slump even when she was tired. She was a proud person—too much, sometimes, what her father called stiff-necked—and she was reserved, gave her friendship and loyalty sparingly.

"Okay, people!" Mr. Marchese called. "Let's have the first pantomime. Lewis? Ferd?"

Lewis—thin, nervous, shy—followed by Ferd—big and stolid—went up onstage. Two unlikely candidates for drama class, but both here because of Rhoda. Jenny sucked on the Lifesaver, resisted the impulse to turn again and stare at the boy in the rainbow suspenders. Had he really been looking at her, not Rhoda?

Rhoda Rivers, best friend, a sun around which many male planets revolved. On Valentine's Day eight boys had each sent her a single red rose. Astonishingly, only a few years before, Rhoda had been a short, bony thirteen-year-old, quick with smiles, smirks, and elephant jokes. Now she was a queen, moving through Alliance High with a constant retinue. Rhoda's hair stood out all over her head, frizzy and shining. She had become quite beautiful and, at the same time, had taken to wearing eccentric clothes.

One day she had come to school dressed all in pink—pink angora sweater, pink harem pants, pink ballet slippers—and she had carried around a stuffed pink rabbit. On another day she wore a striped baseball cap perched on her mass of hair where it rode like a little ship, and on her wrists, like bracelets, candy-striped ribbons tied in bows.

Onstage, Lewis slowly crumpled to the floor where he writhed with an agonized expression, while Ferd twirled his right hand above his cupped left hand. Suggestions came from the class. "Let me touch my native soil." "I can't stand it anymore!" "I'll never get the stains out of these white pants."

Jenny's eyes slid out of focus. Casually she put her arm along the back of the seat, turned ever so slightly . . . and, yes, he was watching her still. He had a mass of curls and beneath—the face of an angel. She put on an indifferent, yet slightly curious expression, as if she'd turned around to study the dark, stained walls at the back of the auditorium: those greasy hand prints, something anthropologists of the future might liken to cave drawings.

Then again she faced forward. Someone must have guessed Ferd and Lewis's pantomime. A new pair were going up onstage. *The face of an angel.* What a remarkable thing to think. What was happening to her? Where was her ordinary reserve and caution? *The face of an angel*—what did she mean by that, for instance? High cheekbones, a broad, shining forehead, a defined nose (a nose that had character), but it was his eyes, blue eyes . . . Even separated by rows of seats, she had seen the blue of his eyes, the blue of a lake or a country sky. *The face of an angel*— how excessive! Surely, she didn't mean that. . . .

"We're next," Rhoda said, nudging her.

Onstage they stood opposite each other, hands raised and flat on the air, then each moved her hands searchingly, as if over a pane of glass. Their theme was "Something came between them." It had been Jenny's idea.

When they came offstage, the boy was gone. And Jenny thought, *Well, no wonder, it's March.*

Chapter 2

"Here, sweetie . . ."* Amelia Pennoyer spread her youngest daughter's fingers on the piano keys.

"Like this?" Ethel asked. At five, she was still chubby, and her hair, somewhere between the color of honey and sand, was combed into old-fashioned shoulder-length corkscrew curls, which Amelia put up in papers twice a week. Of all Amelia's children, this last, she thought, was the gentlest, the one readiest to meet the world with a smile.

Ping . . . ping . . . Ethel banged down on the keys. "Ethel, watch." Amelia played the simple tune. Really, she had very little to teach her. Years ago, as a child herself, Amelia had wanted piano lessons, but her family had not been able to afford them. In the first year of her marriage she had found the upright through a MOVING, MUST SELL EVERYTHING ad. It had cost $100—two of her paychecks—at that time a huge sum. Now the piano was old, the top covered with white water stains, out of tune, and rarely used.

Oh, she had had so many plans: to take piano lessons, to have three perfect children, to go to college nights, to love Frank the same way forever; in short, a master plan for life to be wonderful.

Well, in some ways—those first few years, for instance—it had been so very good: the babies, and Frank, trim then, with all his hair. And that energy! He would leap out of bed mornings, grab her by the foot. "Come on, lazy, get up! Look at that day!" And times he'd get frisky, run all over the house carrying her piggyback.

"Try to push the keys down crisply, Ethel." Memory was a strange thing. Certainly there were memories Amelia could do without. Times she'd yelled at Jenny, the miscarriages before Ethel, the way her father-in-law had died. But, on the other hand, there were so many things she couldn't remember that she wished she could. Sometimes, lying in bed at night, sleepless, she would try to remember the last time she had hugged Gail, kissed her.

She moved restlessly on the piano bench, wondering how much Ethel remembered of Gail's death. She'd only been three. How much could a three-year-old understand? They had told Ethel that big sister went to Heaven, that Gail was with God. Ethel had nodded as if satisfied, but weeks later she asked her mother, "When is Gail coming home?" Now an image came to Amelia—a car scraping Gail off her bike, like a knife scraping butter.

"Today I sang a song in school," Ethel said. "Mrs. Lawret said I was good as television. Did you watch me cross?"

"Yes."

"With the binoculars?"

"Yes."

Pittmann Elementary School, where Ethel had started kindergarten in September, was only two blocks from their house, but the corner of Catherine Avenue and Pittmann Street was a raceway for impatient drivers going to work. Mrs. Young, the crossing guard, a tall, needle-thin black woman, was always on duty, holding back the traffic for the children. She knew every child by name and never took her eyes off them, yet every day Amelia stood on the porch watching Ethel through binoculars. Because . . . because Gail was dead . . . because Mrs. Young might look away for an instant . . . because at that precise moment a car might come down the street, the woman behind the wheel seeing Ethel only through a sodden, drunken haze. . . .

Amelia wiped sweat off her lip. *Stop . . . enough.* No, finish it, finish the picture: Amelia is running down the street, she feels nothing, hears nothing, she is running, flying, flying to rescue, to save, to snatch Ethel from beneath the wheels as she had not been able to snatch Gail. And she is turning to the creature behind the wheel, to the evilness that drank and drove, turning to her and . . .

Amelia's heart raced painfully. And *what?* She had never raised her hand to anyone. Oh, sometimes a swat or a slap to one of the kids, but not this, not this rawness in her, this rage.

"Mom?" Ethel looked up, frowning.

"Keep playing, sweetie."

7

Two years. Tomorrow would be two years. March eighth.

She thought of Gail coming into her bedroom at night, sitting on the edge of her mother's bed. "Oh, Mom, wait till you hear!" Couldn't wait to spill out the details of her day. Sweet, *sweet* the way she'd share things with Amelia. Not like Jenny. Jenny would just look at you without saying a word, making you feel uncomfortable, as if she were creeping into your mind. How different they all were. Gail and Jenny. Vince and Frankie. Night and day, all of them.

The phone rang. Her stomach jolted. *Jenny* . . . *Frankie* . . . Had something happened? What if it were Valerie calling from California to say that Vince . . . Everyone knew California drivers were insane, that on the L.A. Freeway . . .

She picked up the phone in the kitchen. " 'Melia," Frank said. "You need anything?"

"Oh, Frank!"

"Who'd you expect, Johnny Carson?"

Hearing her husband's ordinary, weary voice comforted her. "Why don't you bring home some of those ginger snap cookies Ethel likes?" she said. "Oh, and a quart of milk."

"Everything okay?" he said.

"I was just working with Ethel on the piano." They talked for another moment, then hung up. In the living room Ethel punched the keys aimlessly.

Jenny rode her bike home slowly, taking it easy, not pushing. It was nearly dark, the air crisp. Odd

8

how that thing she and Rhoda had done for drama class kept popping into her mind. *Something came between them.* Then she thought of the boy with the rainbow suspenders. Oh, he was so beautiful. . . . Could he really have been looking at her like that? Nearly eighteen, and she had never had a real boyfriend. Nothing serious. Many crushes when she was younger, then fewer and fewer. Waiting. Waiting. For what? For whom?

She coasted down Jericho Hill. Her mother would have supper for her. She'd study while she ate—as long as her father wasn't home yet. He didn't like people doing two things at once. "If you're going to eat, eat. If you're going to study, study." She squeezed the hand brakes for a red light and realized that tomorrow was the eighth. For weeks she'd been aware of the day coming closer, aware and yet pushing away the awareness. Pushing away the guilt that lay like a hard seed just beneath the surface of her mind. The thought that Gail might be alive today *if.* If she hadn't taunted Gail . . . if she had said at once, *Okay, I'll go to the store.* . . . If she had insisted when Gail finally got peeved enough to start out, *No, Gail, I'll go, you stay and finish baking.* Yes, then everything would be different today. She had always been swifter, speedier than Gail. She had walked faster, talked faster, her temper had been quicker to ignite. She had even done her homework, gotten dressed, and taken showers faster than Gail. And she would have made the trip to and from the market faster. Safely.

Two years.

At seventeen she was already a year older than her older sister ever would be.

"That you, Jenny?" her mother called as she opened the door.

"Jenny, my sister." Ethel was in her pajamas, listening to a record.

"Ethel, my sister."

The house smelled wonderful, tomato sauce and garlic bread. "I'm starved, Mom." She never felt hungry at work.

"I thought I heard sirens." Her mother looked up from the oven. A tall woman with worried brown eyes that always seemed to hold secrets Jenny would never know.

"I saw cars piled up down at the corner."

Her mother's hands flew out. "Not another accident! This street—"

"No, no, I think it was just a traffic jam." She sat down at the dining room table with her food and chemistry book. Her father was working late. In her room Ethel was talking to herself.

Once that had been Jenny's room, also. She had shared it with Ethel and Gail. Now Ethel had the big room all to herself. Well, not exactly, since, in a sense, Gail still occupied it, too. There was Gail's shelf full of glass animals, Gail's out-of-date movie mags stacked on Gail's bureau, and Gail's bed exactly the way she had left it: bedspread wrinkled, stuffed animals across the pillow, and Frye boots lined up at the side. And then, too, there were snapshots of Gail pinned on the wall. Gail as a pretty, chubby baby (looking remarkably like Ethel). Gail, a plump, smiling six-year-old. Gail kneeling in her pleated cheerleader's skirt, her hair falling loose and curly around her face, looking into the camera proudly.

Every morning for a year and a half after Gail's death, Jenny had awakened to see those pictures and every morning something heavy and thick filled her heart. For a long time after Gail died, Jenny had found it impossible to do anything nice for herself. She gave up girls' track, she denied herself movies, TV, ice cream, and even long, hot showers. She knew it was penance for the fight she'd had with Gail. She knew the penance was meaningless, but for months she had been helpless to stop herself from doing, or not doing, those things. Gradually, her life had returned to normal. Rhoda had helped. On the bad days when Jenny couldn't stave off the memory of her last fight with Gail, Rhoda would stay with her, walking sometimes for miles and hours, Rhoda talking, her arm linked with Jenny's. It wasn't that Rhoda said anything special, but that she was there. Once, Jenny tried to thank her. "For what?" Rhoda said. "For talking? I should thank you for listening."

"Enough to eat?" Jenny's mother said now, sitting down across from her.

"Plenty, Mom. It was good."

"How was work today? And school?"

"Okay." Jenny thought of the boy in the rainbow suspenders. That was private. She started telling her mother a funny story about a customer who had turned his thick shake upside down to show how solid it was. " 'You see,' he said to me, 'it's like glue.' And

11

just as he said it, the whole shake fell out *glop*, all over the counter."

But her mother wasn't really listening. She drummed her fingers on the table. "I sent her a red rose," she said abruptly.

"Who?"

"That woman. Montana."

"The woman who—a red *rose?*"

Amelia Pennoyer nodded. "I ordered a single red rose. I told them I wanted it delivered tomorrow."

"Mom, a red rose—that's for love. Red roses are what Rhoda's boyfriends sent her on Valentine's Day."

"It's for blood, Jenny. You know what tomorrow is. I want to remind her."

"Mom—" Jenny looked sadly at her mother. "Enough, Mom," she said softly. "It's been two years. You've got to—" She stopped, not wanting to say *forget*. She didn't mean that exactly, but something like it. "You've got to let go, Mom."

Her mother had caught her hesitation. Strange how, despite their apartness, which Jenny sometimes felt so acutely, they often, as acutely, tuned in to each other's thoughts. "I don't want that woman to forget," her mother said. "I want her to remember the way I do. Every day of her life."

Chapter 3

"**W**ell, fans," the radio voice burbled enthusiastically, "This is Norman Greenberry here to tell you it's a BEAUTIFUL Wednesday morning in our fair city. The forecast is for plenty of SUNSHINE on this EIGHTH day of MARCH and—"

Glancing at her mother, Jenny snapped off the radio. "Thanks," her father said as she sat down next to him.

Amelia stood at the stove, flipping pancakes, her head bent. She wore an old gray-and-yellow housecoat with a loose hem. Nobody said anything about the date, but Jenny knew none of them was unaware. Well, maybe Ethel, but Frankie had looked as if he were ready to smash the radio just before she turned it off.

The sun hadn't been shining two years ago on March eighth.

"Where's Gail?" her mother says, coming in, a shopping bag in her arms. Her face is wet, full of color. "Why'd she go out? Did she wear her raincoat?"

13

"She was baking something, needed cream." Jenny bites her pencil. If x equals 56 . . .

The phone rings. Her mother: "Oh, hello, Frank . . ." In their room, Ethel murmurs to herself. In the kitchen, her mother turns on the radio. Rain spatters the windows.

Her mother comes back. "Jenny, when did you say Gail went out? I've been home nearly an hour."

"She probably met a boy."

"What market did she say?"

"I don't know."

The doorbell. "Who can that be?" Her mother goes into the hall. Jenny flips pages in her history book. Do it tomorrow first period?

"Jenny."

"Yeah?" Not looking up.

"Jenny!"

Going into the hall then, seeing her mother suddenly old, nose gone beaky, eyes sunk back into her head. A policeman standing there. "Jenny, there's been an accident . . . Gail . . . stay with Ethel . . ."

"Mom? Mom!"

She's gone.

An accident?

Her father calls from the hospital. "Gail's in a coma. Stay home with Ethel. The best thing you can do for us right now."

She feeds Ethel, puts her to bed. No use trying to do homework. Sits in the living room, the TV on. Phone again. "Mom?"

"It's me, Frankie. Tell Mom I'm staying over at Burt's."

14

On the TV, kids dancing, wriggling hips, hands shaking in the air. "Milk," someone says. All laugh. An in-joke. "Come home, Frankie. Come home right away."

"I told you, I'm staying over—"

"Frankie. Gail's in the hospital." She tells him what she knows. The policeman. An accident. Coma. Her voice is dry and tight. She hangs up. Why isn't he here now? Why isn't someone here with her? She's all alone. All alone with her thoughts. She wants to cry, can't, hits her fist repeatedly on the wall . . .

Jenny finished her milk, put the glass in the sink, and kissed her mother's cheek. "I'm going now. Take it easy, okay?" She and Frankie left the house together. "How was the concert last night?" she asked as they walked toward the bus stop.

"Okay."

"You don't sound too enthusiastic."

"Oh, Mimi and I had sort of a fight—she keeps pushing me. When am I going to go back to school? She doesn't believe me when I say never. Sometimes she sounds like Dad; he thinks because I'm a mailman I haven't got any ambition."

Jenny patted his blue-gray uniformed sleeve consolingly. "And she didn't even know you in your box factory days."

"Yeah, right. I'm going to sic you on Mimi. Make her realize what a prize I am now."

How odd to think there'd been a time when she was shy with her brother —he'd always been so sleepy-eyed, so distant. "Did you notice how quiet Mom was this morning?"

15

"I did. When that moron said, 'THE BEAUTIFUL EIGHTH OF MARCH' "—he mimicked Norman Greenberry's chirpy enthusiasm— "I felt like punching him right in his radio."

"Frankie, Mom told me something sort of strange yesterday. She said she sent Mrs. Montana a red rose."

"What do you mean?"

"Mom sent her a red rose. To be delivered today."

"Why?"

Jenny leaned out into the street, looking for the bus. "She said red was for blood. I told her, 'Mom, red roses are for love.' "

"I can see her point," Frankie said, sounding almost admiring.

"I can't," Jenny said. "Frankie, do you ever wonder *why*, about Gail? There's no sense to what happened."

"Sure, I've thought about it. It was fate. I believe everything is linked. If I hadn't needed a toothbrush, I wouldn't have met Vic Ramsay in the drugstore last year, so I wouldn't have gone to his sister's party, and I wouldn't have met Mimi. Links. Now what if I hadn't taught Gail to ride a bike?"

"Probably she would have learned anyway. But you didn't teach her. You taught me. Vince taught Gail."

"I remember teaching her." Frankie frowned as if Jenny were trying to take something away from him. "She learned fast, too."

"*I* learned fast," Jenny said. Why did people insist on remembering things wrong about the dead? After

16

her grandfather died, years ago, she'd heard her parents talking about him as if he'd been a blessed old saint. But, alive, he'd been a thorn in their sides, querulous and demanding.

And Gail—her mother had made a shrine out of Gail's part of the room. And what about the special box—sacred box— with all Gail's report cards, a lock of hair, the letter from her cheerleader's sweater, and a cassette tape Gail had made the summer she'd gone to visit relatives in Maine.

Her father generally didn't talk about Gail, but when he did, a special smile would come over his face, as if he were seeing Gail in his mind, and she was so good, so wonderful—perfect, really.

And she—wasn't she capable of the selfsame deception? Only the other day, hadn't she said to Rhoda about something or other, 'Oh, Gail would have had the answer to that!' Conjuring up an image—totally false—of a wise, warm, and loving older sister. But now, all at once, Jenny quite clearly understood what that phrase, *Something came between them*, really meant.

It had to do with her and Gail. Something certainly had come between them—Gail's death. They had never gotten along really well, and now they never would. They were frozen forever with Gail sixteen and Jenny fifteen, bickering and picking at each other. They would never understand each other now, never talk like sisters, never laugh together again, never again have another chance to be kind or loving to each other.

"Sometimes, I think if Gail was still alive, things

17

would be totally different," Frankie was saying. "I don't mean the obvious things. I mean—take me and Dad, for instance. He doesn't get down on me the way he used to."

"I know." Jenny shifted her books. "Things are definitely better, but that's because you graduated high school and got a job."

"That helped, but I'm sure the real reason he doesn't chew me up anymore is because he's basically mellowed out since Gail got totaled."

"Totaled—what a horrible thing to say."

"What do you want me to say? Crashed? Smashed? Wasted?"

"She was killed," Jenny said evenly.

The gray-and-red bus was approaching. "Are we having a fight?" Frankie asked. "Mimi last night? You this morning?"

"I'm not fighting," Jenny said. "I'm a pacifist."

To Nell Montana:

Today is March eighth. I hope you have slept as few nights in the past two years as I have. But I doubt it. Has what you did affected you in any way?

You drank and you drove and you killed an innocent sixteen-year-old girl. Have you given it one thought since then? Do you look at yourself in the morning and know you are looking at a murderer?

Do you know my daughter suffered for days before she died? That wasn't a cat in the street you killed! That was my child. Today is two years, and I still can't rest.

My daughter is in her grave. You should be in jail! Yet you are free. Free to shop, free to go to the movies, free to enjoy yourself. Why hasn't society done unto you as you did unto my daughter?

Sweet dreams, Mrs. Killer.

Grieving Mother

Chapter 4

Seven times that week Jenny saw the curly-haired boy in school. Once, as she was going into the guidance office, he came around the corner at the far end of the hall. "Hello," she breathed. Impossible for him to hear her, but his head turned as sharply as if she'd shouted his name.

Another time, passing the band room, she knew, without any reason to know, that he would be there. The door was open, she looked in, and yes, there he was, working over the big snare drum, head down, drumsticks flying, hands flashing. He was gone, in another world, seeming so totally absorbed she surely might have stopped and stared at him forever without his knowing. Yet in the same moment she passed, he looked up. A smile started, but nothing was said. Still, it was as if the entire day had been meant for that brief exchange.

And on still another day, as people poured out of school in a loud, laughing, and noisy mass, she saw him ahead of her. *Turn around*, she thought. *Turn around. I'm here.* And he did. He turned, he saw her. She told herself to speak. *Hi. Hello! Who are you? What's your name?* But, again, neither one said a word.

Which one of them would speak first? It began to seem like a contest. They passed in the halls, looked at each other, smiled, waited, neither spoke, and they kept going.

At night, in bed, pushing the pillow under her head, listening to the *sloosh sloosh* of passing cars and watching the headlights flash across the ceiling, Jenny tried to imagine their first real meeting, their first words. Someone had to break the ice. How long could they go on just looking at each other? How did it begin with other people? In books and on TV, what did people say when they wanted to meet?

She thought of a movie she'd seen recently. The boy and girl sang in the same chorus, he standing behind her. " *Halleluja, Halleluja,*" they sang. Later, the girl, passing the boy in the hall, said, "You have a lot of energy in your singing." The boy was shy, so he got awkward and stammered, "I do? I do?" His friends punched him and laughed, and the girl, very pretty and appearing really confident, said, "Yes. My name is—" The boy's friends punched him some more, so he'd realize he should tell her his name, too. And then the girl said, "You have a smashing voice." Something like that. And they were off and away.

Well, so she had complimented him, built up his ego, drawn him out of his shell. Was that what Jenny should do? Firmly take the initiative? Was the golden-haired boy in the blue shirt the shy sort? She could say something like, "I feel a lot of energy coming from you." Or, "You should always wear blue shirts." She couldn't comment on his singing voice, to say nothing of his speaking voice. And he didn't have a gang of friends waiting around, waiting to punch him and make sure he got her message. Which, down to its bare essentials, was, *I'm interested. Are you?*

In the library one afternoon, Jenny was studying—supposed to be studying, but she was daydreaming. It was raining outside; the room was dim, feet shuffled, whispers broke the silence, and then she saw him coming through the turnstile, books under his arms, shirt sleeves rolled up. A sharp, blank sweetness covered her. Her eyes fell to her book. *Thus, in the historical mode,* she read. *Thus, in the historical mode. . .*

Steps. A chair was scraped back. She wrote in her notebook, as if aware of nothing. *Thus,* she copied busily, *in the hysterical mud—* Her lips twitched. She dared a glance upward. He was sitting across from her, looking straight at her. The entire dim room seemed to light up. A glow entered . . . a stained-glass window letting in light . . .

The pen hung in her hand, her eyes jumped, unseeing, across the page. *Oh, what a fool I am,* she thought. Nothing like this had ever happened to her before. She couldn't understand how someone, a boy, a stranger, could make her feel so much, could turn her silent and yearning, could take away every ounce of her poise.

He's just a pretty face, she told herself sharply and sarcastically. *Snap out of it, Jenny.* Yet in the next moment she again raised her eyes. And again he was looking at her. And again neither spoke, but only stared at each other.

Later, riding her bike to work, she went over the encounter in the library. "Why didn't I say hello to him?" She bent low over the handlebars, the rain whipping her face. "Or, I could have said, 'My name is Jenny. What's yours?' " In the employees changing room of Hamburger Heaven, putting on her yellow suit, the jacket and wide-bottomed pants, she was still talking to herself. "I'm going to do it. The next time I see him—definitely." She gave herself a confirming nod in the mirror, straightened the yellow cap, and hurried out to punch in.

"Are you late?" Awful Albert said in his wheezy voice, catching her arm.

"It's not four o'clock yet, Albert."

Looking suspicious, the manager released her.

"May I help you?" Jenny asked a customer, taking her place at the counter. Not yet supper hour, and already people were lined up three deep.

Today's special was the Mystery Dinner for kids under twelve. For ten cents over the usual price, their burger, shake, and fries came with a pullout party favor, a plastic puzzle, and an entry blank for a Kids' Sweepstakes.

As always, Jenny started her stint wanting to smile at everyone, to give everyone a little bit of personal attention. As always, the faces began to blur, as did the orders for fries, hamburgers, shakes, Cokes, and pies. Girls and boys in yellow suits rushed around, jostling each other, calling out orders. They dipped the large strainers of frozen, cut potatoes into the vat of boiling fat, slapped frozen burgers onto the grill, swept the floor, and wiped the tables.

Jenny liked the people she worked with. Matti and Phyllis were older, Marylee her age. Matti, who had Dolly Parton curls, and Phyllis with her long, kind face, liked to outdo each other boasting about weekend blasts. Marylee was quieter, worked hard, and could always be counted on to stand in for someone else in a pinch.

"May I help you?" Jenny said for what seemed the thousandth time. She glanced at the clock. Half an hour more. The evening rush was letting up.

"Soda, please." A male voice. She looked up.

"Large or small?" she said, automatically.

"Small." It was him. Only the counter between them. And his eyes were blue, lake blue; she had been right. She turned to the soda machine, put a paper cup under the nozzle, pulled down the handle, aware of him watching her. Every gesture seemed significant; the room blurred, only he stood out. She slid the soda across the counter.

So they'd finally talked. *Soda, please. Large or small?* Not what she'd imagined! She wanted to laugh, bit her lip, smiling. *You have a lot of energy. You have a gorgeous voice. What's your name? My name is Jenny.* "Thirty-five cents, please," she said, efficiently punching numbers on the register.

He handed her a quarter and a dime, dropped the coins into her open palm, and at the last moment their

24

fingers touched. A shock went through her, something warm and vibrant. She leaned toward him, across the counter.

Behind him, a man coughed impatiently. Jenny seemed to come awake, and the boy stepped aside. "Two burgers with everything," the man said, looking up at the big printed orange boards. "Cup of coffee, apple pie."

"Two burgers with everything," Jenny repeated into the mike. When she looked around, the boy was gone.

Chapter 5

"Don't give me that cross-eyed look," Rhoda said. "Maybe you don't appreciate it, but Hamburger Heaven is fantastic preparation for life. I don't have to work," she went on, unperturbed by Jenny's groans, "so I don't. My folks give me anything I want—"

"I know, I know," Jenny said.

"—within reason, of course," Rhoda continued. "And in one way I'm glad. I'd hate to *have* to work in Hamburger Heaven—"

"But it's good enough for the peasants."

"Oh, shut up, Jenny. The point is, I worry about me. I'm so protected. Do you see what I mean? I'm serious, you know."

"Rhoda—" Jenny put her arm through her friend's as they came out of the mall. It was Saturday morning and they'd been shopping for two hours. "I really don't think you should worry. Believe me, Hamburger Heaven is about as far from real life—"

"You're wrong," Rhoda said. "When I was in there last week, it struck me just like real life. A bunch of people grabbing things and screaming and shoving each other around."

"It's really funny you'd say that," Jenny said as they crossed the street. "Nobody screams in your house."

"My point exactly," Rhoda said. "My home is unreal."

"Rhoda, you're going to make out fine in the world. People like you. They follow you. Why should you worry?"

"Look, Jen, sometimes I feel like I'm in a bubble. Like there's a piece of glass around me, something between me and, and reality."

"Why do you think reality is working in a greasy hamburger joint?" Jenny argued. "That's ridiculous. Just because your life is different doesn't make it less real." As she said it, she saw two boys rounding the corner and approaching them. Ferd Govenda and—*him.*

"It's just a feeling I have about myself," Rhoda said. "I see the way you are, and your family, and it makes me feel like I—we, my parents and I—like we're living off in this little ivory tower."

The boys came closer. Now *he* saw her and smiled. "I see what you mean," Jenny said, but she had hardly heard Rhoda. "Isn't that Ferd?" A smile came over her face, brilliant and longing, uncontrollable. "I wonder who's with him. Do you know who that is?" Her voice sounded high and fatuous. Rhoda must see through her pretended innocence.

27

"Rho-da!" Ferd said, stopping. A look of doggy appreciation filled his eyes.

"Hi," Rhoda said, coolly smiling.

"Where you going? What are you two doing?" Ferd said.

Jenny and the boy nodded to each other. He was wearing his rainbow suspenders with a pen clipped to one suspender. He grinned at her, rocked back and forth on his heels, then hooked his thumbs through his suspenders. She smiled at this gesture— *yes, I think you're mighty cute!*—looked away, looked back, the smile growing. Should she say something? Or wait a little longer? Let him speak first? *I like your suspenders. Your eyes are beautiful. Do you want to kiss me, Blue Eyes? Hello, I'm Jenny.*

"Okay with you guys?" Rhoda said.

"Mmm, fine." Something had been agreed on between her and Ferd, something about food . . . a pizza. They walked down the street, clustered together. Ferd—big, thick-shouldered—was ebullient. Of course; he had Rhoda to himself. He'd bought a new baseball glove and continually punched his fist into it to soften the leather.

He—the he of her dreams, the boy in the rainbow suspenders—walked next to Jenny. Their shoulders touched lightly. All at once, he tugged one of her braids, the merest tug, a little playful pull. Her cheeks were already hot; now her face, her neck, and her ears heated up. She blew her breath up on her face, then mischievously reached out and snapped one of his suspenders. *How about that? You tug my braid.*

I snap your suspenders. He laughed out loud. Maybe they'd go on this way forever, not talking, only signaling everything with their eyes.

In the pizza place a wave of warm, spicy air greeted them. "This way." Rhoda led them to a booth near the back. "Sit here, Ferd." It was all arranged. Jenny and Rhoda on one side, the boys on the other. Jenny directly across from *him.* Would she be able to eat? To do anything as normal and ordinary as bite into a pizza, chew, swallow, wipe her lips, take another bite . . .

"Girls, what'll you have?" Ferd said. "Order anything you want."

"You're not paying for us," Rhoda said.

"Aww, Rhoda," he whined. "I didn't know you were one of those libbies." He chucked her under the chin.

So Ferd was something of a fool. Did that mean, since *he* was with Ferd, he was also a fool?

Rhoda leaned back, looking a trifle bored. "I'll leave it up to everyone—whatever you guys want."

"What do you think?" he said to Jenny.

"We can each pay for our own. It's fairest."

"That's fine with me."

Aha, a conversation! Real talk, at last. And so practical, so down-to-earth. *We can each pay for our own. That's fine with me.* She took back her doubts about his mental stability. Excuse me, pardon me, you're not at all Ferdish.

"I'm paying for Rhoda," Ferd said in a loud, aggressive voice.

Rhoda smiled faintly. "No, you aren't."

"Aww, Rhoda—"

Poor old Ferd. Jenny's heart softened toward him. He was in love with Rhoda, and, of course, it was hopeless.

The pizza came, the drinks. Rhoda described their shopping trip, Ferd talked baseball. *He* ate his pizza, watching Jenny all the time. She rolled up her pizza, nibbled a corner, put it down. No appetite. What had Rhoda said earlier? That she, Jenny, lived in the real world? Something like that. Yes, yes, very real, to sit woozily across from a boy she'd been dreaming about and still not know his name!

She reached for the cheese sprinkler; so did he. The sprinkler tipped over. "Go ahead, take it," he said.

"No, you take it."

"That's all right—go ahead."

"You were there first."

"Hey, Rob," Ferd said, "Rhoda doesn't believe I once did six hundred sit-ups."

Rob. "Is that short for Robert?" Jenny asked.

"Robin. I don't know your name."

"Jenny. Short for Jennifer."

He took the pen off his suspenders and wrote her name on a napkin. Upside down she saw that he'd written it incorrectly.

"It's Jenny with a *y*," she said.

"*J-e-n-n-y?*" She nodded, and he wrote it again. "Jenny," he said, as if tasting her name. "Jenny, I saw you working in that hamburger place, Jenny. Is that when you work there, on Tuesdays?"

"Yes, and Thursdays, and Sundays all day."

"That's why I didn't see you there on Friday."

Had he gone looking for her? Silence again, and then they both spoke at the same moment.

"You first—"

"No, you—"

"But I took the cheese shaker. You take the conversation."

"I was going to ask—you're new in Alliance High?"

"I used to live here. I moved away a couple of years ago to live with my father in Binghamton, after my parents divorced." They were leaning toward each other across the table. "My sister, Jade, stayed on with my mother. But now Jade's moved, my father got married again, and my mother's alone. So I came up to live with her."

She nodded. "I see." She saw that he was kind, that he cared about his mother being alone. She imagined his family—father a look-alike, sister someone exotic (Jade! what a wonderful name), his mother brave but lonely.

"Do you have a boyfriend, Jenny?" Rob asked quietly.

"What are you two whispering about?" Rhoda said.

Ferd raised his hand for the waitress. "Check," he called importantly.

Jenny shook her head. "No boyfriend. Do you—"

"No," he said quickly. "No one. I'll call you tonight. Is that all right?"

"I'll be home."

31

"I'll call you. What's your last name?"

"Pennoyer, we're on Pittmann—"

"Pennoyer? Your name is Pennoyer?"

"Yes, and you're—"

"Montana," he said, he said, slowly.

Then it was her turn to repeat. "Montana?"

They stared at each other.

"A red rose," he said finally. "Would you know anything about a red rose?"

Jenny stood up.

"Where are you going?" Rhoda called after her. "Jen—"

She pushed open the door. The high glare of the street struck her face.

"Wait," Rhoda called behind her. "*Jenny!*"

Chapter 6

"**S**nap to it, Jenny." Awful Albert gave her a shove. "Customers waiting!" Sweat rolled off Albert's face, and there were orange half-moons under his arms. Jenny grimaced and moved away. Rushing past, Phyllis patted her. "Don't let Awful get to you," she whispered hastily.

Jenny packed a tray with burgers, fries, and orange sodas for a man in a white leather jacket. She punched numbers on the register, pulled out the bill, handed it to the man. All night long the name Montana had woven through her dreams. And when she woke up, it was the first thing she thought. Montana . . . Montana . . . Montana . . . Was it possible she'd misunderstood. *Know anything about a red rose?* No, it was certain.

"Thank you for coming to Hamburger Heaven. Have a nice day." Automatic words. Automatic smile.

"Little lady—" The man in the white jacket was back. "You gave me five dollars too much."

"Oh! Thank you."

"Good thing I'm honest," he said in a loud voice. He looked around to see if anyone was noticing. "Five dollars too much."

Awful rushed over. "Is anything the matter? What's the problem?" he panted.

It had not been a good day for Jenny. She'd splashed soda on her uniform, given a cheeseburger to a woman who had ordered a fishburger, and didn't even see a very small man, a midget actually, waiting for his order. "Am I being discriminated against?" he said. Jenny winced. Why did all the dissatisfied customers have such loud voices?

Late in the afternoon, Rob came in. The early supper-hour customers were straggling in. He was wearing a short khaki slicker and Bean boots, a businesslike outfit. He came right up to Jenny. "I want to talk to you. What time do you get off?"

"Five o'clock."

"I'll wait."

"You can't just hang around here." She glanced at Awful. He was famous for sniffing out anything "personal"—all such things being strictly forbidden on page twelve, paragraph three, line five of the Hamburger Heaven Employees Handbook.

"I'll have, ah"—Rob glanced at the menu—"a burger and a glass of milk." He sat in a far corner, stretched out his legs. Every time Jenny glanced over, he was just sitting there, tapping the table, not eating.

At exactly five she punched out. In the employees' room she stuffed her uniform into a plastic bag. Outside, wind lashed the trees. The sky was overcast. She walked through the parking lot and, as she came around the side, Rob fell into step beside her. "Why'd you run away yesterday?"

"I didn't run away."

"You ran away from me," he insisted. "Why?"

"Why do you even ask? You know the answer. Our names," she threw at him. "Pennoyer. Montana."

There was a moment of silence, then he said, "Jenny. Rob."

They turned onto a quiet street, small one-family houses and little stores crowded together. It had begun to rain. In the light from the houses, his face was vivid. His eyes shone. For a moment she forgot everything, forgot their names, forgot her sister and his mother and her mother—forgot it all.

The rain fell hard, wetting their heads. They ran for shelter under a tree, leaned there panting and laughing. "Jenny?" he said, and they came together, held each other tightly, their faces pressed together. "I'm sorry," she whispered. "I'm so sorry." A car approached; headlights shone through the falling rain. They broke apart, resumed walking. A wind came up, and the trees groaned.

"There's no month like March for weather," he said.

"I don't like March," Jenny said. "My sister died in March."

A space grew between them. She walked faster, walked ahead of him. After a moment he caught up with her. "I'm sorry—I didn't think."

"It doesn't matter. It just shows how impossible it

would be for us. That's why I didn't hang around yesterday. It's pointless. We can't be friends."

"I don't believe that," he said in a stubborn voice.

"Look." She hesitated for a moment, then said flatly, "Your mother killed my sister."

"It was an accident, Jenny." A roughness, a tremor, came into his voice. "Something happened —something terrible, but—"

"Your mother was drunk," she said. It had to be said.

"She had *one* drink."

"What difference does it make!"

"One drink." He said it again. "Anybody could have one drink. She was at a party, and it was raining, like now. She doesn't drink, she's not a drinker."

Jenny held her peace. They hurried along, hunched against the wind and rain.

"What does it have to do with us?" he said. "We're us, we're not our families." She shook her head, felt somehow much older than he.

Taking her hand, he said, "Say my name?"

"What?"

"Say my *name*."

"Why?"

"Just to hear you say it."

"Rob." she said. "Rob Rob Rob RobRobRob . . ."

The way he was looking at her! A giddiness overtook her. He grabbed her, she knew he would, a bear hug, both arms around her, trying to wrestle her into submission. She swung the plastic bag, hit him on the legs and the back, broke free. She ran, and he ran after her, both of them splashing through puddles. He caught her at the corner. "Got you!"

"I let you."

They walked again. He put his arm across her shoulder. She loved it, and said, "Look, we *can't.* It's still no good."

"I hear you, but I don't believe you. I have so many feelings about you already, I can't believe we're not going to be friends. At least we could give it a try," he said. "What do you think will happen?"

They kept walking, long easy strides, the way she liked to walk. *What will happen? Nothing catastrophic, Rob, nothing dramatic. Only I will never be able to say your name in my house. I will not be able to bring you in, as Frankie brings Mimi. You won't eat with my family, you won't meet my parents, you won't exist at all for them. And I don't know how I can see you and not remember what I'm remembering now, that it was your mother who—*

"Tell me about you," he said. "I want to know about you."

"I have two brothers, a sister." *Once I had two sisters.* "My grandfather died. Do you have a grandfather?" Safe subject.

"Yes, and a grandmother."

"Do you like them?"

"I love them both very much."

How sweetly he said that. How easily and unselfconsciously. She remembered once, years ago, sleeping over at Rhoda's and suddenly saying, "I love you, Rhoda." And then being incredibly embarrassed. But she had meant it. She still loved Rhoda in a special

37

way, and she loved her grandfather, Carl Pennoyer, who had been dead for almost five years, and her sister Gail, and . . .

I'll never be able to tell Gail now that I love her, Jenny thought. They had spent so much of their time fighting. She had hated Gail passionately, often.

At the corner of Pittmann she said, "This is where I turn." She held out her hand. "Good-bye, Rob."

"I'm not saying good-bye," he said. "Where's your house?" And he kept walking with her.

In front of her house she stopped again. "This is the end of the line."

He took her hand, squeezing it painfully. "I'm not giving up, Jenny. Don't go in. Let's walk some more. I want to talk to you some more. Do you mind the rain? Here, take my slicker."

"I like walking in the rain, but my feet are wet." As if that were all that kept her from staying with him.

"Change your shoes, put on your raincoat, and come on out again," he said. "We have to talk. We have to settle this."

She understood that "settle" meant to do things his way. The streetlight at the corner gleamed blue. She looked at him, at the high cheekbones, the broad, smooth forehead. "I don't think I should come out. It doesn't make any sense."

"What are you afraid of?"

She shook her head impatiently. "There's too much against us. It's not as if our families had a little insignificant spat."

"Our families don't even know each other. Look,

just tell me this: Do you want to go in your house and not come out? Do you want me to go away? Is that what you want, Jenny? Is that what you really want?"

"Rob, I'm sorry, it's just no use. I don't see how . . . I can't be your friend. I just can't," she said. She hurried up the steps and didn't look back.

Chapter 7

"**H**ello?" Jenny said.

"Hello! Do you always answer the phone in your house? Can I count on it?"

Saturday morning. The first time in a week they had spoken. She had told herself, *Avoid him. It can't be, therefore there's no point in even speaking.* But, in fact, every day she had spoken to him silently. And what had she said? All sorts of things. Important and unimportant. Big and small, silly and serious.

There are so many things I'd like to know about you; everything, actually. For instance, what foods you like, are you going to college, do you take school seriously (I do), and as far as that goes, is it possible that blue is your favorite color (it's mine) because I see that you have three different blue shirts.

Do you like music? (I saw you in the band room . . . is that serious?) How about reading? What are your favorite TV shows?

40

I see that you're taking AP Math. So am I, section two. A good thing we're not in the same classes, that would be too hard. . . .

Yesterday when I walked into school, you were right there. You shouldn't look at me like that! I didn't make up these rules; it's just the way things worked out.

Today I saw you down the hall ahead of me. You knew I was behind you, but you didn't turn. I don't blame you, what's the use, I won't speak to you. No, I refuse, because it will only start up again if I do. This way is better, Rob, I speak to you in my mind and you can't answer, I say what I want without having to watch for those sensitive spots. If we were together, it would be impossible for me to mention my sister, or you your mother. . . . No, this way I have some hope that I'll get over you; get you out of my system, as they say. Yes, get over this—this whatever it is . . . Can it be love? Can it really be love? Yes, it's just what's called "love at first sight," but now I've had my second and third and even more sights of you and I still am in this stupefied state . . . yes, that's the truth of it. . . .

You see, Rob, how I can say all sorts of things in my head that I wouldn't ever say out loud. Not because I'm ashamed, but simply because I'm the sort of person who doesn't say everything aloud. And you're the sort of person, I think, who says a great deal, who's emotional and full of feeling and not reluctant at all to let it out. We're quite different. Does that mean we're really perfect for each other? I

41

*shouldn't even think things like that! Danger-
ous. . . .*

"Are you busy?" he was saying on the phone. "I
thought we could go for a walk—"

"No." A flood of words in her head and now this
stingy "no." Her mother was ironing in the dining
room, but that wasn't the only reason for her brevity.
If once she began talking to him, let herself go, how
would she ever stop?

"How about a bike ride?"

"No."

"Drive in the country?"

"Don't, please—"

"I want to see you."

No reply.

"Do you want to see me at all? I mean, even a little
bit? You do, don't you? Tell the truth!"

"Yes," she said.

"I knew you did. Jenny . . ."

"Yes?"

"Just wanted to say your name. You know what I
thought when I first saw you? That day in the auditorium? I thought, Oh, God, who is that sweet, beautiful
girl? What did you think when you first saw me?"

"I can't say now."

"Is there someone there who you don't want to
hear?"

"Yes."

"Otherwise you would tell me, wouldn't you?"

"Look," she said softly, "there's no point—"

"Jenny, don't keep saying that. There is a point—
us. I refuse to believe—"

42

She broke in. "Why are you calling me today? All week we didn't even say hello."

"I was waiting for you to speak first," he said.

"I won't. Because we just can't—"

"We can," he said. "We can, we can, we *will*."

"You are so stubborn," she said. And was glad for his stubbornness, glad it was equal to her own.

Chapter 8

Sunday, Rob was waiting for Jenny when she got off work.

"Hello." He took the handlebars of her bike and wheeled it. "Are you going to tell me to go away?"

"Would it do any good?"

"None at all."

"Then I won't say it."

"Round one for me."

She cut her eyes at him. "Oh, so this is a contest."

"But there's going to be two winners," he said quickly, laughing at her.

"Are you always this sure you're right?"

Before he could answer, a car pulled up ahead of them, the door opened, and something was thrown out on the shoulder of the road. Rob and Jenny just stared for a moment, then saw it was a kitten.

"Oh, *hey*," Jenny yelled as the car pulled away.

The two of them ran toward the kitten, the bike bouncing clumsily between them. "Drop it, drop the bike," Jenny said. The kitten staggered toward the middle of the road. Rob got to it a moment before Jenny and picked it up. A car passed, beeping its horn at them. The kitten was tiny, all white, except for its ears which were little chocolate peaks.

"It's a baby, just a baby," Jenny said as the kitten clawed into Rob's arm. "But I bet it knows what happened. Do you think so?"

"Definitely." Rob petted the kitten. "Animals sense all kinds of things."

"What are we going to do with it?" Jenny said, picking up the bike.

"Take it to the ASPCA, I guess."

"You know what happens to most of the animals there? Especially kittens. There are so many of them, they keep them for a while, and then—"

"You're right, you're right. We won't do that. Poor thing, it's shivering."

"I'll make it a bed in my saddle bag." She lined the bag with her uniform. "Come on, baby." But the kitten, digging in, flared its ears and refused to be detached from Rob's arm. "Calm down, you don't have to, if you don't want to." She ran her hand down the kitten's milky back. "We've got to do something with it. I'd take it home, I'd love to, but my mother can't even be in the same room with a cat without her face puffing up."

"I'll take it home with me, then," Rob said. "Would you like that, Snowball?"

45

Jenny groaned. "Not Snowball, please."

"What's wrong with Snowball?"

"Oh, nothing, I suppose, only I like more dignified names for animals. Why stick silly names on them that you wouldn't put on a person?"

"You name him, then."

Jenny considered. "What would you think of Carl? It was my grandfather's name."

"I like it." Rob put the kitten on his shoulder inside his jacket, with only its face showing. "What's little Carl doing?"

"Getting ready to sleep, I think." She rubbed the kitten's nose. "He is sweet."

"You'll have to come visit little Carl," Rob said. "You're responsible for him, too, you know. We saved him together."

"Mmm . . ." Jenny said.

"Mmm, what?"

"Rob, what are we doing? What are we saying? You know I won't come see Carl. I can't go to your house. This is crazy. I thought we settled—"

"We didn't settle anything," he said. "We never agreed on anything. All we've done is not talk for a week. That's not settling things."

"But nothing has changed," Jenny said.

"How can you say that?" Rob rubbed the kitten's ears. "Here we have Carl, our first child. He wants his parents to love each other."

Jenny rolled her eyes. "Rob, that's either not very funny, or icky. Sentimental."

"Aren't you sentimental?"

"No, I don't think so, not at all. It doesn't mean I

don't have feelings. I just think there's a place for them."

"I bet you don't even cry in movies," he said.

"Do you?"

"My eyes get red, but I try not to let the tears fall. Why are you walking so far away from me? Come closer, I have something to tell you. I've been thinking about us. A lot. Jenny, all we have to do is forget our last names."

She understood. Become last-nameless. Drop Pennoyer, drop Montana. Blot out their families, their connection to their families; embark on their journey together as souls alone. Two atoms in space, meeting, falling into the same orbit.

She looked at him. "It can't really be that simple."

"Why not? Look, let's begin right now. Until we get to your house, you're Jenny and I'm Rob. No other names. No other people. Only the two of us. Here we are, we've met, and as soon as I looked at you, I thought, 'Who is that sweet, beautiful girl?' And you thought . . ."

How could she resist? She didn't want to resist. And it was only for the moment, just playing, pretending like two kids, that they could have what they weren't supposed to have. "I thought, 'Who is he? He's got the face of an angel!' "

"I don't know what to say to that." He pushed the bike with her. "Is that what you really thought?" She nodded. "I don't think I can live up to that," he said. "Now I want to know things about you. Start at the beginning."

"I was born on a dark and stormy night . . ."

47

"No names, but all the details, please."

". . . in a strange place called a hospital. I took my first step at the age of nine months, and my first word was—"

"Wait, wait, you're going too fast. When were you born?"

"August fifteenth."

"Now there is a coincidence for you! I'm January fifteenth. Coincidences come in threes, so look sharp for the next two."

It was this way, light and playful, all the way to her house. As they turned onto Pittmann, a few drops of rain fell.

"God is cooperating tonight," Rob said. "He knows you like walking in the rain, and He knows I want you to be happy so you won't go in your house and leave me the way you did last week."

She didn't want to leave him. And yet, where was she heading if she stayed? It was unreal to pretend. No, it was impossible for them to be friends. She'd known it from the moment she heard his name. Impossible. The word separated itself in her mind, the "im" so small, the "possible" so large. "Where are your rainbow suspenders?" she said. "You're not wearing them tonight."

"Where are your sneakers with holes in them? Where are your braids? I like your braids."

Holding Carl he followed her as she walked the bike to the back of the house and put it into the garage. "This is the car my father is working on for me," she said, turning on the light and indicating the black Dodge Dart. "I'm paying for it while he works on it." She got behind the wheel and started steering.

"What are you doing?" Rob said, getting in on the passenger side.

Jenny gave an embarrassed snicker. "Playing car. Where would you like to go, sir? Jennifer's Chauffeur Service at your service."

They leaned against each other, shoulders touching. "What's your dad doing with the car?" His head turned; his words were in her hair.

"Fixing the rusty parts . . . fenders and . . ." He was so close. How good his skin smelled. "I should go in," she said in a faint voice.

"Not yet."

She stroked the cat's tiny head. "Rob . . ."

"Jenny? We don't need last names, no last names, just us."

Just us. Could they? Could they really? She thought of her sister. His mother, her mother. She roused herself. *What are you thinking of, Jenny?* "I'm going in. I really have to—"

"Don't go, Jenny!" He gripped her hands. "It's just *us.*"

Just us. Oh, why not? Would it be so wrong? How could something she wanted so much be wrong? She freed her hand. "I'm going in," she said. Then, looking at him: "Wait. I'll be right back."

Chapter 9

"**H**i, Dad," Jenny said. Her father was watching a special news report on TV. Dan Rather looked worriedly into their living room.

"Just get home from work?" He leaned forward, paying attention to Dan Rather.

She heard her mother and Ethel talking in the bathroom. "Hi," she called, going past to the kitchen. She made a sandwich, poured a glass of milk. So, she had made a decision. After all her arguments, her hesitations, her insistence that the past lay between them like a wall. After all her "we can'ts," all her "it's impossibles." What had happened to all that resolution? Rob. It came down to that. Him. Rob.

Her mother walked in carrying Ethel. "Want to smell my hair?" Ethel asked. She was in pajamas.

Jenny obliged. "Smells yummy." Was she being disloyal to her family? But what if it was just for a bit . . . who knew how long they would last? No, be honest. There was something real there, already something deep. More than a "crush."

50

Ethel sat down at the table. "Can I have marsh-mallows in my hot chocolate?"

She was going out to walk with Rob. Did that mean she was choosing him over her family? How melodramatic. Why make such a big thing of it? Why not just say she was choosing to let their friendship grow, to see where it would lead them.

She rinsed her plate and glass. "I'm going out for a walk with"—she barely hesitated—"with a friend."

If her mother were to look out the window now she'd see Rob standing outside, waiting, but it wouldn't mean anything to her. Not unless Jenny said, *That's Rob Montana.* She wouldn't say it. No last names. *Just us.* "I'll see you later."

"Who did you say you were going out with?"

"Oh . . . a friend from school."

"Anyone I know?" Her mother handed Ethel a cup. "Careful, it's hot."

"No, it's . . . Robin." She put an apple in her pocket and went out.

The rain never really came. A spattering, then it stopped, then another spattering. Jenny and Rob walked, holding hands and talking. "This is the beginning," Rob said.

"Let's always be honest with each other," Jenny said.

"I wouldn't lie to you."

"I know. I mean it in a different way. I mean no little lies, not even little nice things to make each other feel better. Do you think we can be that way?"

"We can try," he said. Carl rode inside his jacket and Jenny told him about the real Carl, her grandfather. How, when she was small, he took her to the park every day. How, for so long, he was the center of her life. "I never missed a day without seeing him." The bad time came when she was thirteen. "He was eighty-three, getting kind of cranky, I suppose, and my parents thought—well, it was complicated. My brother Vince came home married and we were awfully crowded. My parents got the idea the best thing would be for Grandpa to go into a home. He didn't want that, so he left. And I left with him."

"You ran away?"

"I suppose you could put it that way. I think that's the way my parents felt, but tell me this: How can an eighty-three-year-old man run away from home? Anyway, we went to the farm that had been *his* grandparents' place, and we tried to live there. One night, it was autumn, getting cold." She steadied her voice. "He went outside and I found him in the morning under the apple tree. He was dead. They said he died of exposure."

"Did he get confused? You know, that age—"

"I don't think so. I thought about that a lot. I remember once he said something to me about how every living thing wanted its bit of space—well, him, too. He couldn't see living in a home. That just wasn't living to him."

"So he was brave," Rob said.

"Yes, that's it exactly."

He stroked her hand, and she was grateful and comforted because he had understood, and because he let them walk in silence for a while. And she knew he had really been listening to her, had heard even beyond her words, because the next thing he said was about some friends of his he wanted her to meet.

"They're in their seventies, and they're wonderful. They're always busy and always together. Just the way I think people should be when they get old. She's Margie and he's Art. They were my sister's friends first."

If they were careful they could talk about their families. She spoke of her baby sister, her two brothers; he of his father—"He was always hugging me when I was little"—and his sister, who sang with a band, Sandy Big Feet. "They're trying so hard to make it. They play any gigs they can get, anywhere, the sleaziest, smallest club. They'd play a Boy Scout picnic if they were asked. All the time we were growing up, the moment Jade walked in the house, she'd turn on the radio, listen for hours. She knows thousands of songs."

They talked about their plans for the future. "Don't laugh," he said. "I want to be a kindergarten teacher."

"Why would I laugh?"

"You know, a guy wanting to be a kiddie teacher. Some people think that's a little strange. But I think little kids are neat. They're still free spirits and a person could really influence them for good."

"It's funny," she said, "you love kids—well, I do, too—but I really love old people. I love their faces and hands especially."

He wanted to know what she intended to do. Work

with old people, of course, she said. And she wanted to know if he'd had a lot of girl friends. Then he wanted to know why she wanted to know that. And she said she was just curious. And he said, Would she be jealous if he told her he'd had dozens? She denied this vehemently in one breath and said "Yes!" in the next.

"Okay, what would you think if I said—none?"

"I'd think you were a liar! I'd think you already forgot that we said we'd be honest."

"Okay, the truth." He held up a single finger.

"One? Only one girl friend? What was her name?"

"Roberta."

"Rob and Roberta? I don't believe this."

"My eighth-grade love. Roberta Whizninski. She gave me a kiss behind her father's barbershop. I wanted more, more, more. Poor Roberta. I was always trying to grab kisses off her. One day she said, *Bug off!* Wow. She just pushed me away. *Bug off!* I was crushed. After that I liked other girls, but somehow . . . I remember this one time I was going down the street and I saw a girl I liked coming toward me. Patti Fletcher. It was summer, a hot summer day; I was wearing sandals and cut-offs. As soon as I see Patti, I start strutting, sticking out my chest, swinging my arms, the whole bit. Throwing back my shoulders. Patti's smiling. Fantastic! She's smiling at me, I can't believe it. She's never even given me the time of day and here she comes, big terrific grin for me. And I'm looking at her and thinking, Oh, oh! I manage to say, 'Hi, Patti,' and she says, 'Hi,' but it's sort of choked because by then she's laughing really hard. Why? I could *not* figure it out. Then on the way home, some kid yells at me, 'Hey, you're unzipped!' You know what, Jenny? I didn't go to school for a week."

"Oh, poor Rob! Oh, that's terrible! That's a terrible story."

Later, as they turned back toward her house he said, "I want to give you something. Something from Rob to Jenny. To show that we're—"

"We're *what?*" she said.

"Us. Just us."

"I don't need anything."

"I know that. I want to, though."

"Don't get any ideas about rings," she said. "I don't like rings. I like hands, plain hands." She seized his hands and inspected them. No rings, no bracelets. Hers, the same.

"Okay, I won't give you a ring, I'll give you an elephant."

"I'll keep it in the garage with the Dart," she said.

The next day, meeting outside the school, he snatched her lunchbag and dropped something into it. "What's that? Give me back my lunch."

"You'll see." He held it out of reach and ran through the swinging doors. A couple sitting on the stairs watched as Jenny grabbed Rob and tickled. "No respect for private property," she cried.

"I thought you were a pacifist." He squirmed with laughter.

"I am; my motto is don't shoot, tickle."

He relinquished the lunchbag, and she took out a

small china elephant with trunk upraised and four pink feet. "Is it all right?" he asked. "I told you I'd give you an elephant." .

She smiled and stroked its gleaming white back. "Maybe I won't keep it in the garage, after all."

Chapter 10

In the library Rob sat down next to Jenny. "Hi," he whispered.

"Hi," she whispered back.

He moved his chair closer, touched her foot with his foot. "I got my schedule changed."

"Shh!" someone said.

Rob unclipped a pen from his suspenders and wrote on a piece of paper, "Gym, fourth period. Fifth period, lunch with Jenny."

"You have fifth-period lunch now? How'd you manage that?"

He tapped his forehead significantly. "I did it. Did you notice the weather?" Behind his propped-open notebook, he whispered, "We might never have another great day like this until *next* April. Want to cut out?"

"Where would we go?"

"Anyplace else."

Outside she saw the blue sky, and trees, glossy and swaying in a light wind. So it was April—she'd nearly missed the change, even though Ethel had said, "Jenny's got a rip in her blouse. April Fool!" *April.* She felt suddenly released, glad that March was gone.

She shoved her books together. "Let's go!" He clipped his pen back onto his suspenders and closed his notebook with a clap that made heads turn. They walked fast, through the library, out the turnstile, and into the hall. "We'll meet outside." He continued to whisper conspiratorially.

At her locker she pulled on her corduroy jacket and, after only a moment's thought, dropped her books and closed the locker.

Rob waved from across the street near the candy store. Jenny ran to meet him. "How'd you get out so fast?"

He did a little toe dance. "We're both wearing sneakers with holes in them today. Another one of your major coincidences."

They walked, almost skipped along, holding hands. "Let's move fast," Rob said, "so they don't catch up with us criminal elements. Jenny, I bet you've never done this before. Do you think your character is going to be damaged forever by contact with me?"

"Don't take so much credit. I've skipped plenty of times. What do you think I am, a wimp?"

"I think a lot of things about you, but wimp definitely is not one of them. You haven't asked me something important."

"What's that?"

"Think, Jenny. Here's a little hint—meow?"

"Carl! How's Carl?"

Rob looked happy. "Carl is fantastic. He sleeps all

night on my bed and chews on me in the morning to wake me up."

"So it was all right that you brought him home?"

"Sure, I've always had a cat or a dog. I left my dog at my father's when I came up here because Dammit is more than half Dad's. Just as well, since I don't think Carl would want to share my bed with Dammit."

"How'd he ever get a name like that?"

"We were going to name him Spot—something really original—but what happened was, when we were training him, Dad would say, 'Dammit, do it here!' 'Dammit, aren't you ever going to get trained!' Before you know it, pup comes every time anyone says Dammit. So Dad said, 'Well, that must be his name.'"

"Your father sounds nice."

"He is. Hey, I've got a great idea." He pulled her into a phone booth at the gas station on the corner. "Let's call my father. Operator? Hi! I want to make a collect call—"

"Isn't he working?"

Rob shook his head. "He works second shift. . . . Dad? It's Rob." He moved slightly, bumping into Jenny, leaning against her. "Sure, I'll tell her . . . Uh huh . . . right . . . she did? Great! . . . Hey, Dad, I have somebody here who wants to say hello to you."

"Rob, no," Jenny whispered.

"Her name is Jenny," he went on, "and she's terrific. The most terrific girl I ever met." He pushed the phone into Jenny's hand.

"Hello, Jenny," she heard his father say. "Is that it—Jenny?"

59

"Yes, Jenny," she said, making a face at Rob. "Hello, Mr. Montana."

"Well! Rob gave you some build-up."

"You, too," she said.

"How's the weather up there, Jenny?"

"Oh, it's beautiful."

"Well, enjoy it while you can. Before you know it, summer'll be here, and then it'll be too hot."

"You're right," she said. Then there was one of those silences you can almost feel. Rob's father cleared his throat. "Well, Jenny, let me speak to that boy of mine again."

She handed the phone to Rob, pushed open the door, and stepped out. "Why'd you do that?" she said when Rob came out. "I don't know your father. It was really embarrassing. I must have sounded like a fool. I didn't know what to say."

"You couldn't sound like a fool."

Jenny rolled her eyes. "Stick around."

"I plan to," Rob said. "My actual, secret master plan is to stick to you like Super Glue. You're never going to get rid of me, Jenny."

"Oh, no?" She gave him a shove that caught him by surprise. Before he could recover she was off and running. Rob was right behind her. Maybe she would never stop. She would run, and he would run, and they would go on and on and on . . . At the corner, at the stream of honking cars, she came to an abrupt halt.

"I didn't know you could run like that." Panting, he put his arm across her shoulder.

Jenny smiled smugly. "You may be Super Glue,

but I am Super Feet. Where shall we go? Blue Lake Park?"

In a small grocery they bought seeded rolls, a hunk of Gouda cheese, milk, molasses cookies, and apples. On the bus to the park they sat in back and ate the apples.

The park was deserted, the beach empty, the lake green, not blue, and mushrooms were growing in the sand. It was cooler here, and they decided to have a fire while they ate. "I think this is illegal," Jenny said, feeding twigs into the small blaze. "We'll probably spend our twilight years in adjoining cells." She sat down, took out her jackknife—the one that had been her grandfather's—and cut the rolls in half and sliced chunks of cheese. They passed the carton of milk back and forth.

"We'll take our trash out with us," Rob said. "I cannot litter. My Boy Scout training. Every summer when I was a kid, for a couple weeks I went to Boy Scout camp, even went after I wasn't a Boy Scout anymore."

"Was it fun?"

"I loved it. How about you—did you go to camp?"

"No, none of us did. Oh, maybe my older brother, Vince—"

"Vince—he's the handsome devil?"

"Right."

"And he's how old?"

"Twenty-four."

"And he's going to be a father."

"Uh-huh." Valerie had written:

Dear Family, I'm pregnant! If it's a boy he's going

61

to be Vince, Jr. If it's a girl, it will be Gail. . . .

"Okay," Rob said, "I'm getting these Penn—" He broke off. "Getting all this straight. So maybe Vince went to camp, but Freddie didn't?"

"Frankie. I guess after we all started coming, my folks didn't have the money. We'd play with each other summers, and I'd visit my grandfather—"

"I thought he lived in your house."

"Yes, but he had his own apartment, remember? Down in the basement. It's Frankie's now. When I was little I thought of it like visiting someplace else. It was so special. Grandpa's house. I'd go there every day. And then there was the baby to look after, so there was always plenty to do. Gail and I took turns—"

She stopped, busied herself with the fire. Gail's name had just popped out. Wrong. No last names, no mention of mothers, and no mention of one sister. The dead sister. But how difficult it was. How could they be totally open, honest, if there were so many things to avoid? Like being in a swamp and having to avoid quicksand.

She leaned her chin on her knees, poking at the fire. "I have a cousin Ernie who used to tell me stories about the quicksand that was going to get me if I wasn't careful. How it was going to suck me down, down, down. I'd scream, he said, but nobody could help me.

"I believed Ernie. He was older than me. And I was terrified for the longest time if I saw even a bit of sand. Even sand in a sandbox. My mind would flash, *Quicksand.*"

He rubbed her head. "Oh, this is as bad as my zipper story."

"I never told anyone, not even Grandpa. Then one day I said to myself, *I won't let that quicksand get me.* And I made myself go into sandboxes and stuff. I was little when this was happening. It seemed so real to me."

"Little kids have all kinds of stuff going on in their heads," he said. "People think they're just merry and happy, but it's not true."

"I don't think Ethel is afraid of anything," Jenny said. "At least it doesn't seem that way to me."

"Ethel—she's the youngest, right? Does everyone spoil her?"

"More or less. We try not to, but you know . . . and especially since—" Again, she stopped. She had almost stepped into the quicksand.

"I've always been sort of spoiled by everyone, too," Rob was saying. "Not that *I* think I'm spoiled, but Jade used to say I got stuff—privileges, love—she didn't get. She always told me I was so protected, but I don't think so. I remember plenty of things going on between my parents—fights they didn't want me to know were happening. But I knew. I would be lying in bed, listening to them talk in the kitchen. I'd be drowsy, sleepy, and then all of a sudden my whole body would become—stiff . . . just *tense;* my legs would shake they'd be so tense, because something in their voices, some change would tell me they were fighting. I used to think, *Their beanpole voices.*"

"What a funny thing to think."

"I know, it seems funny now, but then it just

seemed the right thing. I must have been five or six, and somehow saying that—*Their beanpole voices*—seemed the exact way I felt. Maybe because I've always hated green beans, and my mother insisted I eat them. Sometimes I'd sit at the table saying 'Beanpoles, beanpoles, beanpoles' as fast as I could. And after a while it would be 'Meanpoles, meanpoles, meanpoles.' But they were never mean to me. They were very loving, just not to each other.

"What I started to tell you was about this one time they were fighting. They had their beanpole voices. I was right there. My mom had her hands on my shoulders, talking to my dad over my head. First I'd hear her say something, and then I'd hear him. And I didn't know which one to love, which one was right, which one was wrong.

"That bothered me a lot. I wanted *someone* to be right, *someone* to be wrong. You know how kids are. Who's the good guy? Who's the bad guy? I still have this tremendous enthusiasm for cowboy movies—"

"I know, I know," Jenny said, "you can always tell the white hats from the black hats."

"Exactly." Rob laughed.

"Do you realize what we've been doing?" she said. "We've talked about practically nothing but our families."

"I was thinking the same thing."

"We said no last names, just Jenny and Rob, but we're like a couple of turtles, carrying our families around with us on our backs."

They finished the cheese, shared the last roll, and, leaning against each other, ate the whole bag of cook-

64

ies. How frightened she'd been, Jenny thought, every time one of them mentioned their family; afraid they'd ruin everything. Instead, all afternoon it had gotten better and better.

They kept the fire going and sang songs. Their hands played together, twining, untwining, twining again. Something had changed between them. It was as if by talking about their families they had separated out the bad parts—Gail's death, the guilt and anger, her mother sending a red rose of blood to his mother—and packed them into a little box, while the rest—their childhood memories and the stories about their brothers and sisters—were in another box, a big box. They could talk easily about the contents of that big box. Maybe they could even talk about the little box as long as they were careful to put everything back inside, close the lid, and remember who they were—Jenny and Rob. *Just us*.

The sun was going down. "I suppose we should go," Jenny said.

"I guess so."

Neither of them moved. Rob poked at the embers. "I wish we could always be like this." He looked at her.

She wanted to kiss him. She wanted him to kiss her. She moved toward him, put out her hands. He was smiling a little. "Hi," he said, and for the first time they kissed. And kissed. And kissed again.

In a while, they got up and packed their things, covered the fire, and, hand tightly in hand, walked out of the park to the bus stop.

Chapter 11

"Where are you going?" her mother said as Jenny passed through the living room.

"Out. Downtown."

"Meeting Rhoda?"

"No. Just going to do some shopping." Uncomfortably, she planted a little blue newsboy's cap on her head. It was Saturday morning and she and Rob had arranged to meet at one o'clock in Messenger Square. Every day they'd been seeing each other in school, eating lunch in the cafeteria or outside on the stone wall near the parking lot. After school they met again and walked to Jenny's job or just walked and talked, arms around each other, bumping shoulders, and stopping on quiet streets to kiss.

"Did you bring your laundry down to the basement?" Her mother was wearing her Saturday cleaning outfit—old jeans and one of Jenny's father's shirts.

"Right. And my room is clean. I vacuumed, did the windows, too. Anything else?" Jenny said, showing a willingness to put off going out that she didn't really feel. She disliked being evasive with her mother. She could never mention Rob, but so far in accounting for her time she had managed to avoid outright lies. When her mother asked where she'd been, and why, even on days she didn't work, she came home so late, Jenny could say truthfully enough, "I was in the library," "I was downtown," "I met a friend and we got to talking."

"Don't come home too late," her mother said now.

"I won't. Are you and Dad doing anything special tonight?"

"Her mother laughed. "Like watching TV?"

"You ought to go out more."

"Oh, your father's always so tired—"

"Well, he should do it for you." On impulse she hugged her mother, who remained almost stiff in her arms. No, they weren't huggers in their family; they didn't even touch that much. It was from Rob that Jenny was learning how to hug. His hugs were big and warm, bear hugs, generous and unself-conscious. Jenny wondered if her parents had ever hugged for pure joy, the way she and Rob did. Not being put off by her mother's stiffness, she hugged her harder. "What's this, Valentine's Day?" her mother said, but her face softened and her cheeks got pink. "You're growing up, aren't you, Jenny?"

Downtown, Rob was waiting for her near the fountain, one foot up on the stone rim. Jenny came up quietly behind him, put her arms around him, and squeezed.

"Hello!" Rob turned, smiling. "You look pretty."

"Were you waiting long?"

"Couple hours."

"Rob! We said one o'clock." Then she saw his smug smirk and raised a fist. "You're teasing me again."

"I can't resist, you're such an easy mark. What should we do today? Should we go to a movie?"

"Maybe." Jenny smiled privately.

In the darkness of the movie house they sat close and kissed endlessly.

After the movie they were both hungry. "Fried chicken," Jenny said.

"It's fattening."

"What are you worried about?"

"I wasn't always this slender sex object you see before you, Jenny. I used to be fat and funny-looking." Jenny laughed. "True," Rob said. "I only lost weight last year when I gave up eating supper."

"How about the funny-looking bit?"

"How about it? Look at this nose."

"But, Rob, you're beautiful. Remember what I told you I thought when I first saw you? The face of an angel—"

"You're embarrassing me."

"You love it!"

"I have to admit . . ." He snickered. "Did you really mean it?"

"You just want to hear me say it again. Who said girls were vain?"

They were still laughing when they sat down in the fried chicken place, but oddly, a memory came back to Jenny at that moment like a shadow in her mind. It must have been those words, *The face of an angel.*

Angels were the souls of the dead. And the memory was about Gail.

"Are you okay?" Rob said.

"I just remembered something awful." She picked up a chicken leg, put it down. "It's making me feel sick just thinking about it."

"What is it?"

"You'll think I'm terrible."

"Don't try to second-guess me. Just tell."

She took a sip of water. "It was a long time ago, maybe nine years ago. We were at Blue Lake and Gail and I were in the water, and—I tried to drown her."

"Why?" Rob said.

She shook her head. "We were fighting over a rubber tire. We were always fighting. Gail pushed me under. When I came up, I jumped on her and pushed her under and—I remember distinctly—I wanted to keep her down. I wanted to drown her."

"You were just a kid. Kids think things like that. You didn't do anything."

"I did," Jenny said. "I *tried*. And now she's dead."

"Jenny, *you* didn't kill her," he said, and then, apparently hearing himself, picked up the plastic fork and dug into the box of chicken. A silence fell between them. They ate with their eyes down. *Are we always going to blunder this way?* Jenny thought.

"Hi, over there." Rob pushed her foot with his. "You haven't eaten very much."

"I ate at home. Here, you can have the rest." She pushed her box across to him.

"You'll make me fat again."

69

"I'll still love you."

They smiled at each other. Jenny sighed. The crisis was over.

It wasn't always that easy. A few days later, leaving school, Rob said, "I want to ask you something. The night Gail went out, was there a reflector on her bike?"

Jenny stiffened. "Yes," she said briefly. *Let it drop, Rob.* But their ESP wasn't working: he kept after it.

"Was she—Gail—wearing dark clothes?"

"Jeans, a red shirt. What's the point?"

"It was dark, rainy. She must have been hard to see."

"She wore a yellow half slicker over her jeans."

"I wish you'd meet my mother," he said abruptly. "You'd see she's not a monster." The weather had turned cool. All the new leaves were turning and shivering in the cool wind. Jenny buttoned her jacket. "Come up to the house," he said. "Let's visit Carl."

"Rob, I don't want to meet your mother."

"She's not home, Jen. She works, remember? I'm not talking about meeting her today. Just sometime. Will you come up?"

"All right," she said reluctantly.

Walking into his home, the first thing Jenny saw was a straw knitting basket with a half-finished sock hanging out. On a table, a vase of silk flowers and framed pictures of Rob and Jade. "Is this your sister?" The same forehead, the same nose. He nodded. "She's really beautiful."

She followed him through the apartment. Pictures on the walls, magazines scattered around, colorful little rugs everywhere. A warm feeling. The house of a woman, a mother; the house of Rob's mother.

"Here's my room," he said. Drumsticks lay on top of a wicker basket heaped with clothes. On the floor were magazines, records, and a bowl filled with apple cores. "A little messy." He picked up a jersey and pitched it into the basket. Jenny looked at the books stacked on a table near his bed. *36 Children. Why Children Fail. A Very Special Child.*

"Come sit with me." He patted his lap.

She smiled, hung in the doorway, couldn't escape the thought that this was his mother's house. All the things they didn't want to talk about were, in this place, too close to the surface. What if his mother walked in now? What would Jenny say? How could she even face this woman who had run down Gail? She grew more and more uncomfortable. "Rob, I'll wait for you outside." Before he could answer, she was out the door, down the steps.

A few minutes later, he came out. "I had to feed Carl."

She looked at him closely. "Mad?"

"Why?"

"Because I ran out."

He shrugged. "I pushed you into coming up. It wasn't fair."

"Oh, it wasn't that bad." Now she defended him to himself. "I just didn't feel at ease."

"Let's forget it. It's okay."

71

Chapter 12

"**T**his is my friend, Jenny, that I've told you about," Rob said.

"Hello," Jenny said, smiling. Art and Margie Chapin sat across from each other at a round table, their heads identically yellow-white, working on papier mâché vases. "I'm glad to meet you, Mr. and Mrs. Chapin."

"Call me Art." A small, compact man, he showed purple gums in a brilliant smile.

"Do you see anything you like, darling?" Margie was taller, thin, with bright brown eyes.

Jenny went around the room, looking, touching, admiring. Every available surface was covered with papier mâché vases, boxes, lamp bases, and bowls, all painted in bright primary colors and glazed with varnish. Margie and Art supplemented their Social Security selling their handiwork.

"Don't buy anything just because you're here," Art said when Jenny picked out a small diamond-shaped box painted Chinese red.

"Oh, no, I love it." Fleetingly she thought of buying a box for her mother. It would lead to questions, though. *The Chapins? Who are they? How did you happen to meet them?* And of course Rob's name would have to come in. *Robin? Is this the Robin you mentioned? What did you say her last name was?* (Her? Last name?)

"I like your friends," she said when she and Rob left the Chapins. "Let's go see them again."

They did go visit Margie and Art again, and then, since it was just across the street from Rob's house, they ran up to see Carl the kitten as well. Each time she was in Rob's house, it was easier for Jenny, easier to stay there, to stay longer.

It was a good time, a time when everything seemed nearly perfect, when every day began and ended for Jenny with the thought of Rob. "I feel left *out*," Rhoda said one day. A comic wail of deprivation, but serious, too. "I want to be in love, too!"

They were in Rhoda's room, sitting on a bench in front of the dressing table. "Half the guys in school are in love with you," Jenny said, "and you say that."

"Oh, they're idiots. I don't ask them to follow me around. I'd rather feel the way you do." Her hand hovered over the lineup of tubes, pots, and jars of makeup. "How did you choose so right?"

Jenny worked on the left side of her face: mascara, eye shadow, blusher, lip gloss. "You know very well I didn't choose. The first moment I saw him—"

"Yes, it's so perfect. Really fairy-tale stuff, and even better that you're star-crossed, that your families hate each other."

Jenny stared at her face, the left side glamorous, the right side familiar and usual. "I'll give you star-crossed," she said, sticking out her tongue and crossing her eyes.

One night when Jenny's father was home, Mimi came for dinner, and everything was somehow lovely. Because of Mimi, Jenny thought. She brought a calmness to their family circle. She wore big tortoise-shell glasses and had silky, wheat-colored hair. She had eased into their family in a natural way, and came and went without fuss.

After supper, Jenny and Mimi did the dishes. "Gail and I always used to fight when we did the dishes," Jenny said, getting a fresh dish towel. "Do you and your brother fight a lot?"

"Well . . . yes and no. It really seems ridiculous for me to fight with him. I'm twenty years old; it's crazy to fight with my little brother, but there are times. . . He's the prince of the house, you know," she said in her calm, accepting way. "It's not his fault. My mother doesn't let him do anything. No, Jenny, don't let me get started on that. Really, it brings out the worst in me when I talk about my family." She scrubbed a dish with the orange sponge. "Does that sound awful? You're very lucky with your family, you know. I can't talk to my mother the way I can to your mother. She's so much under my father's thumb."

Jenny was silent for a moment. Did everyone look at other families and see them as better than their own?

"Cat got your tongue?" Mimi smiled at her. "You know what, you look different. I can't figure out what

74

it is. Are you doing something different with your hair?"

"No, it's just the same." She had a strong desire to tell Mimi, *I'm in love; I'm in love, too, just like you.* "Mimi, did you fall in love right away with Frankie?"

"You mean when I met him at Irene Ramsey's party? No, no. I didn't really get to know him that night. He hung around me, saying how much he liked my green dress and how pretty I was, and—"

"Frankie said that?" Jenny laughed. "I can't imagine Frankie—"

"Oh, he was really coming on to me. You should have heard him. He actually said something like I was the girl he'd been waiting for all his life."

"Oh, no. What a corny line!"

"I thought so, too. I thought, *Big act!* Just goes to show how wrong you can be about people."

When they joined the rest of the family in the living room, Jenny's father started asking Mimi about her plans. "What'll you do when you finish community college?"

"Well, that's just a two-year degree. I want to go on and get a regular four-year degree. Probably a Bachelor of Science."

"You have ambition. I like that."

Frankie put his legs across Mimi's lap. They were sitting on the couch. "She's really lazy, Dad. A good-for-nothing. She's just buttering you up with all that talk about getting a degree. She'll go to work on Mom next. Watch out, Mom!"

Jenny's father turned on the TV. There was a special on called *Say Good-bye.* "What now?" her father

75

said. In a whispery, hoarse voice, Rod McKuen told them about all the animals that were disappearing from the earth because they didn't have enough land and food. Halfway through the film were pictures of men clubbing fat white baby seals.

"This is sick," Mimi said. "I can't watch!" But all of them sat there, watching the slaughter, until Jenny couldn't stand it anymore and left the room.

Chapter 13

"Come on, Rob, let's go."

"What's your hurry, don't you want part of this sandwich?"

They were in his house, Carl on the table. Jenny bent over, dangling a strand of hair in front of the kitten. "You've already eaten two sandwiches. You're going to get fat."

He moaned. "Jennifer!"

"I didn't mean it that way." She kissed him.

"You meant it, Jenny."

"Didn't." Kissed him again.

"Am I getting fat?"

"Don't be crazy. You're not *skinny*, but—"

"Oh, so I'm not *skinny*. What's the opposite? *Fat*—"

"Idiot. Fathead. Oops!"

He pounced on her, wrapped his arms around her. "Say something else. Put your foot in your mouth a couple more times."

She struggled, stepped on his foot, and broke free.

He chased her, and they ran through the house, screaming like a couple of kids. He caught her in the kitchen again. "I'll tickle you," she threatened. "I'll tickle your fat belly."

"You know what I do to girls like you?"

Flushed with laughter, half-kissing, half-struggling, neither heard the front door open.

"Hello, what's this?" A woman in dark pants and a striped tee shirt stood in the doorway.

"What are you doing home so early, Mom?" Rob smoothed down his shirt.

"My usual time." She held out her hand to Jenny. "Hello. I'm Nell Montana."

Automatically, Jenny shook the offered hand. It was small, warm, covered with silver rings. More than once she had tried to imagine this moment, face-to-face with the woman her mother called Mrs. Killer. Tried to imagine what she would say, how she would act: proud, reserved, but articulate.

"Mom, this is my friend, Jenny"—Rob hesitated and finished—"Jenny Pennoyer."

His mother looked straight at Jenny. The same blue eyes as Rob. "Pennoyer? Are you related to other Pennoyers?"

Jenny's mind failed her. Her arms felt limp. On the floor the kitten chased a bit of dust. "I'm Gail Pennoyer's sister," Jenny blurted.

Nell Montana's eyes grew larger, shone with shock and surprise. Jenny's own eyes felt small, fuzzed over. She wanted to shut them, shut away the sight of this woman. "I better go." She moved toward the door.

"Don't go." Nell Montana put her hand on Jenny's arm. "I want to talk to you. I want you to give your mother a message, tell her something for me. Will you do that? Your mother sends me things. She writes me letters. Sit down, please sit down, stay a moment."

Unwillingly, Jenny sank into a chair.

Nell Montana dug a cigarette out of her pocket. "God, what a day. I need something to drink."

Jenny's heart thumped erratically. This was unreal, a scene from a TV drama, but, somehow, she was in the middle of it. *A drink . . . is that what you need? I've often wondered what sort of person you are. I can't imagine my mother drunk. I won't say she's a saint, she certainly takes a drink now and then, but drunk? No, that's something else entirely. I hear the girls at work talking about being bombed out of their minds, and I don't think that's so funny, either, but all the same they're mostly girls. I mean, it's not an excuse, but they are younger, and I guess they don't think about some things, like someone coming along when you're driving . . . but you're a woman, and that's the part I don't understand. And you're Rob's mother. That's the other part I don't understand. Because Rob is so special, and he must be that way at least partly because of you. . . .*

"I better go," she said again. But again Rob's mother protested.

"No, stay. Let's talk. Let's talk like people. I'm frazzled—end of day, end of work. I'm not always this hyper, am I, Rob? You kids want something? I'm going to have a cup of hot tea."

Rob sat down next to Jenny, pressed his foot

against hers. There was an awkward silence as Nell Montana poured a cup of tea. "You sure you don't want something?"

"Nothing. Thank you." Above the table a framed motto read, "Keep on truckin'—around the corner it might be different."

"I'm not mad at Rob for bringing you here," his mother said, sitting down across from them. "Maybe it's even a good thing. I think I can talk to you, Jenny; you have sympathetic eyes. But do you know what I really wish? I wish that was your *mother* sitting there where you are. She has never let me talk to her. Oh, I don't blame her. I understand. I'm the mother of a daughter, too. I know how I would feel if—" She added sugar to her tea and stirred it round and round. Her eyes became red-rimmed, and red splotches appeared on her cheeks. She lifted her teacup with shaking hands. "When is my life going to start again?" she said. "When is it going to be all right again?"

Don't tell me, I don't want to hear this. Jenny's nails curled into her palms.

"Mom," Rob said, "don't get started—"

"I *will* get started, Rob," Nell Montana said in the same passionate way Jenny had heard him say things. "I will. Don't say *don't* to me. Here's Jenny Pennoyer in my house! Here's the daughter of the woman I need forgiveness from! Here's the sister of that poor girl. Gail. You see, I know her name. Of course, I know it! I don't forget. I don't forget anything. I live with it. I live with what I did every day of my life. Do you understand?" She stroked Jenny's arm, a soft touch that struck Jenny as unpleasant.

80

"I suppose my son is right," she said. "I shouldn't get started. People don't like emotion."

"Jenny's not like that," Rob said.

"In my whole life I never willingly hurt anybody." She bent forward. "Then one night, I'm driving home from a party, I'd had a drink, and I'm feeling good, I'm singing a little and thinking about things. Not much of anything, and then—"

"Mom—" Rob said.

"No, let me, let me talk. You want to know something, Jenny? You want to know the *irony* of it? Rob's *father* is the one who likes to drink at parties. Oh, yes, he does. All the times I've said, 'Pal, I better drive because you're half-seas over.' And then that one time— I don't drink. Not hard. Just a friendly drink or two at a party. I don't get smasheroo. I wasn't smasheroo that night. I had a drink, yes, maybe I had two drinks, but not smasheroo. It was just—the alcohol affected my timing, that's what they told me. Just affected it, and it was dark and raining, and so I didn't see her until the last—"

Her voice dropped off. She put her head down on the table. "Oh, God," she whispered.

"Mom." Rob rubbed his mother's bent back. "Mom—"

"I'm sorry." Nell Montana sat up. Again she touched Jenny's arm. "Did I make you uncomfortable? I'm sincerely sorry, but as Rob's father would say, I'm nearly always sorry for one thing or another. My life seems to be a series of sorrys. Sometimes my entire life appears to me to be one big word in the sky—S-O-R-R-Y."

Jenny's hands were freezing. All this emotion, all this talk. In her house there was emotion, all right, but it was reined in, tight, under the surface.

"Are you okay?" Rob said to her in a low voice.

She held out her hands to him, and he rubbed them between his own.

"Hey—" Nell Montana put on a smile. "It's real nice to see young people in love. Are you two in love?" She looked from one to the other and lifted her teacup. "I toast you. Rob and Jenny. Young love. It's probably the best thing we have left in this mean old world. When I came home and saw the two of you it reminded me of days gone by when Rob's father and I. . . Did I ever tell you, honey, the main reason I married your father?"

"Sure you did," Rob said.

"Well, I'll tell Jenny then. It was his name. Montana. I always wanted to stand out and it appeared to me that my name, Nell Smith, was an impossible barrier to achieving anything great in life. Please remember that I was fifteen. How old are you, Jenny?"

"Seventeen."

"Seventeen, and already quite wise. I see it in your eyes. Wise eyes—and they are judging me."

"No, no," Jenny said, but it was true. She had never met anyone like Rob's mother and sitting there, listening and watching, she was trying to put together the pieces of the puzzle that was this woman.

"Well, so there I was, fifteen and dinky Nell Smith, when who rides into town—he really did, on a Harley-

Davidson cycle—but this golden-haired boy named Pete Montana. First I saw him, and then I heard his name. That was the clincher: *Montana.* I said that name a thousand times every night, and it was never enough. Then I said *Nell Montana* to myself, and I saw how having the name Montana would make me someone." She laughed. "Anyway, we got married, and you notice I didn't name my kids Betty and Bob. I thought long and hard over their names. But I hope you love my Robin for *more* than *his* pretty name."

Despite herself, Jenny laughed. Maybe Rob's mother was a little talkative, but she was nice, very nice. And for that moment, looking into the blue eyes so much like Rob's, Jenny forgot everything. Forgot, because it hurt to remember. Forgot, because remembering was the past. And this moment in the kitchen, the three of them in a coziness of family feeling that quickened her heart, this moment was now. This was her time, the living moment of her life.

Chapter 14

"**T**omorrow is our anniversary," Rob said. He sat across from her in a booth. "Two months since we saw each other in the auditorium. Do you want to do something special?"

It was Sunday; Rob had showed up at work just as she got her lunch break. "What I'd love to do is get up really early, maybe five o'clock, even before the sun is up, when everyone is still asleep, and go for a long walk. And while we're walking, we'll eat an entire loaf of hot Italian bread from the all-night bakery."

"We'll do it," he said. "You know what *I* want to do that's special? I want to call you at your house and talk to you. I want to come visit you and hear your parents say, 'Oh, hello, Rob, Jenny's waiting for you.'"

Doodling on a place mat, Jenny drew two little stick figures looking at each other. She began to feel tense. He'd brought this up before, but she couldn't just spring him on her parents.

"I don't like this feeling that we're sneaking around. My mother knows about us now—"

"That was totally accidental, and we are *not* sneaking around." They stared at each other for a moment.

"All I mean is, if you don't tell your parents about me, one of these days someone else will. You know who turns out to be in my bio class? A cousin of your brother's girl friend."

"Mimi? How do you know that?"

"His name is Holtzer, same as her name, isn't it?" Jenny nodded. "Well, I heard him talking about his cousin Mimi one day. So I just figured— And he knows me, and probably knows your name. And we're always together in school."

"I see what you mean." She wrote "Rob" under one stick figure, "Jenny" under the other, and linked their hands.

"Maybe I could meet your folks with a paper bag over my head. Just to get them used to the idea that there's a guy in your life. I'll be the mystery guest."

"They won't have to see you or hear you. They'll love that."

He took the ballpoint from her. On the place mat over "Rob's" head he drew a balloon and inside wrote "Wilt Thou Marry Me?"

"Yes, I Wilt," Jenny wrote back in a balloon over the Jenny figure, "Someday."

Then Rob drew a fourposter bed with two little stick figures lying next to each other, their feet turned out. They were still holding hands. Along the bottom of the bed, he wrote, "Just Married."

"They look chilly." Jenny drew a quilt over them. "Their room looks a little bare, too." She added a tipsy-looking chair and a lopsided bureau. Rob put a frame on the wall in which he lettered HOME SWEET HOME. Then he crossed out the second HOME and wrote JENNY.

"I want to kiss you," he said. "Do you think your boss would mind?"

"Don't know about Awful, but I'd mind."

"Because of where we are?" She nodded. "Then I'll think a kiss," he said. "You, too. Look at me, and I'll look at you, and we'll imagine we're kissing. How is it?"

"Wonderful," Jenny said. "Probably the best kiss you ever gave me."

After a moment he said, "My mother asked about you. She liked you."

"I hardly said two words."

"Those two words impressed her. She's been talking about you ever since."

"Rob, she hasn't."

"Yes, she has. She thinks you're fabulous-looking, like something out of the Arabian nights. And that you're smart; wise, she says."

"This is embarrassing." Was Rob trying to build up a lot of good feeling between her and his mother? He didn't have to work so hard at it. The fact was, she had liked his mother, and under other circumstances . . .

"She wants you to come over for supper sometime."

86

Jenny crumpled her napkin. One thing for her to meet his mother, but this! "You can't force things, Rob. I'm not going to your house for supper."

"I'm not trying to force anything, Jenny. I'm trying to make things better for us. Which is why I want to meet your people."

"I told you I have to talk to them first."

"When are you going to do it?" She frowned. "You don't want to, do you?" he said.

"That's the kind of question where you think you already know the answer, so why ask?"

He looked grim, stood up. "I'm going to get a drink."

"Why don't you make that vodka or gin?"

He stared at her, walked off. She spread a wet spot on the table with her finger. Didn't he know that she wanted everything out in the open, too? But he didn't seem to recognize the depth of her parents' feelings about what had happened. Why was he acting so thick? Did he really think he could whistle and smile and charm his way into their hearts as if he were anyone's son?

He came back and sat down next to her.

"Why are we fighting?"

"Oh, I don't know, Rob. I don't want to! I'm sorry about what I said. . ."

He nodded. "Let's forget it. Want some?" He offered her his strawberry shake.

She shook her head, turned the links on her watch strap. "You know, if things were different, I'd really be glad to visit your mother. It's just—I can't be at ease with her. And my parents—that's a whole other problem."

"I understand," he said quickly. Did he? To begin with, there was a difference in the way she felt and the way he felt about what had happened to Gail. The point being, it was her sister. Then, though she knew he thought it was tragic, he also thought it was something people had to learn to live with, all of them: her parents, his mother, her.

Like her mother, she tended to brood, to chew over things. Rob was good for her precisely because he didn't. His personality was basically optimistic. He was always convinced there was a way, no matter what stood in front of you. That's why he kept harping on her parents.

He was like those Israelites who believed they could bring down the walls of—what was the name of that town?—by blowing on their horns. *Sure, guys, we can do it.* She could see him saying it and tooting away, while she'd be standing by, shaking her head at the sheer craziness of shattering a wall with a tinny horn.

Joshua fit the battle of Jericho . . . that was it. Jericho. They used to sing that in music class in junior high. And then the last line popped into her mind: *And the walls came tumbling down.*

Chapter 15

Rob and Jenny were sitting on the stone wall outside the school. On the lawn a group of people were playing Frisbee, and from the opened windows on the second floor the band could be heard banging out "Pomp and Circumstance." Rob bit into a hard-boiled egg. "What have you got to eat that's interesting?"

"Peanut butter and lettuce."

"Weird. I'll try it."

"Give me a bite of your egg."

They leaned on each other, exchanging food from their lunch bags.

"Talk to your parents yet about my coming over?"

"I want to catch them in the right mood." She raised her face to the sun, sighed. "It seems when my father is feeling benign my mother looks tired, and when my mother is feeling chirpy, Dad either isn't home or he's rushing around doing things."

"Maybe I should just appear. I'll come over to-night, knock on your door, and politely say, 'Hi, is

Jenny in?' And then . . . who answers the door in your house?"

"Whoever's closest."

"Okay, suppose it's your mother. 'Hi, is Jenny in?' She says, 'Yes, who should I say?' I say, 'Her friend Rob.' And she says, 'Come on in, Rob.' And I follow her in and then—um, you're there and you say, 'Mom, this is Rob Montana.' "

"Ahhh, yes," Jenny said. "And then I explain how Robin turns out to be a boy, and the other little detail is his last name, did you catch it? Montana, as in Arizona."

"Okay, your parents are a little shocked, a little upset, but then they calm down. We say we're going together—you know, very simple, boyfriend and girl friend, and, uh, we just wanted to get things, uh, out in the open and, you know, we'll probably talk and your parents will see that I'm not Frankenstein's monster, and that's *it*," he said.

She looked at him. *Oh, Joshua.*

"So what do you think, Jen?"

What should she say? What if he was right? It would be wonderful! And how would they ever know if they didn't give it a try? "Okay," she said.

"We'll do it?" His face lit up.

She felt scared but glad. "I know you're right. We've got to make the break sometime." They loved each other—nothing could change that—and so something had to give. It wasn't going to be her and Rob, so it would have to be her family. Her family! She thought of each one separately. Who could she count on? Ethel? Sweet Ethel, she'd love Rob, but she was

90

a kid. Frankie, then, but he didn't have much influence with her parents. No, it was her father and her mother Rob had to get past. Her father's stubbornness, her mother's grief and anger. *Oh, Joshua,* she thought, *get out your horn and start tooting. This ain't going to be an easy wall to bring down.*

Her father was home for supper that night, and Mimi came, too, wearing a flowered scarf tied around her forehead. Jenny was quiet, preoccupied with how to bring Rob into the conversation. Wouldn't it be wise to prepare them a little bit? *Mother, Father, have you noticed I've been quite busy lately? There's this special person* . . . no, no, too stuffy. Be more natural. *Mom and Dad, there's someone I'd like you to meet, a friend of mine* . . . too vague, get to the point. *Parents. You don't know this, but I have a boyfriend who, it just so happens, is coming over tonight* . . . not bad, but a little crisper. Get down to the nub of the matter. *Folks, I have a boyfriend you are not going to be too happy about. His name is Rob Montana* . . . On the other hand, being blunt might alienate them. Maybe, after all, she should be more subtle, lead up to it gradually?

But how?

Mimi came to her rescue. "Mrs. Pennoyer," she was saying, "last week you promised to tell me about how you and Mr. Pennoyer met."

"You mean that time on the Erie Canal path?"

"What time?" Her father looked up from buttering a piece of bread.

"You remember, Frank. The very first time we

met. I was with Glenda Sherman—"

"Who?"

"Frank!"

"He's teasing you, Mom," Jenny said. She liked the look her parents exchanged.

"It was a beautiful spring day," her mother said. "Glenda and I were walking on the towpath when these two boys came along. One was tall and slim, I think his name was Ernest—"

"Ernie Camber," Jenny's father supplied.

"See! You do remember."

"Of course I do." He winked at Mimi.

"We all stopped and talked. Of course the other boy was your father," she said to Frankie. "I didn't think too much about him."

Ethel pulled at her father's sleeve. "This is a story about you and Mommy?"

"That's right. A long time ago when Daddy was a young buck."

"He was very handsome," Jenny's mother said to Mimi. "You should have seen him. He had all his hair then, and this way of walking . . ." She stood up for a moment and rolled her shoulders. It made them all laugh. "And such eyes," she said, sitting down. "Am I right, Frank?"

"Dad's blushing," Jenny said. "No, you are, Dad. Did you like Mom right away?"

"I certainly did."

"Well, I didn't like you," Amelia said. "Not then."

"You didn't like him?" Frankie sat up, looking interested. "Why not?"

"Because of the way he was looking at me. Of

course, I could tell he was interested—I guess you could call it that."

"I guess you could," Jenny's father said.

"But he had a very superior look on his face. Macho is what you kids call it now. We didn't know that word then. But that's what it was. As if he was doing me an enormous favor just by talking to me. And I was, well, sort of superior myself. I figured . . . I didn't want a fellow to be humble, but I certainly wasn't in any *need*."

"You had other boyfriends?" Jenny asked.

"Oh, certainly." A look of young delight appeared on her face and Jenny imagined her mother as a girl of nineteen—tall, full of pride, jaunty, and pretty. "Anyway, these boys, your father and Ernie, invited themselves to walk with Glenda and me. Well, we're talking and your father is telling me all about himself. You know, building himself up? He's telling me all his plans, right, Frank?"

"It's your story." He leaned back, sipping coffee.

"We came to the end of the path where Glenda had left her car and he, Frank, said to me right out of the blue, "So when are we going out on a date?' "

"I saw what I wanted."

"And he called me 'Melia, as if he already knew me really well. I looked at him and said"—Jenny's mother cleared her throat—"I said, Excuse *me*, Mr. *Penny*, or whatever your name is, but I don't remember saying I would go out with you.' And then I hopped in the car and rolled up the window tight."

"Oh! Poor Mr. Pennoyer," Mimi said, patting his arm.

"No, Mimi, that's not the way it happened at all," Frank Pennoyer said. "She asked *me* to go out with her. I couldn't believe it! I hardly knew the girl!"

They were all laughing when the doorbell rang. "I wonder who that could be," Jenny's mother said.

"I'll get it," Ethel said, hopping off her seat.

"I think it's for me." Jenny followed Ethel into the hall.

"Hi," Rob said as she opened the door. He looked very fresh, as if he'd just showered. His hair was damp and curled tightly. He was wearing an open-necked, deep-blue shirt.

"Who is this?" Ethel said.

"I'm Rob, scout. Are you Ethel?"

"How do you know my name?" She looked at him, frowning, hands on hips.

"Magic powers," he said. "And"—he put his finger to his forehead—"you are five years *old!*"

Jenny gripped her sister's shoulders. Rob was so confident and relaxed, *joking*, while she was all nerves. "Look, guys, can we play games another time?"

"You're hurting me," Ethel said. "*Jenny!*"

"Sorry, Eth," she said distractedly. "Go on in, will you? I want to talk to Rob alone." She knew how Ethel hated to be shoved, but she pushed her anyway. "*Go.*"

The child went slowly, paused at the door, looked back at Rob, and said, "Maybe I don't like you."

"Well, I like you," Rob said. Ethel didn't answer.

"Let's get it over with," Jenny said. As they walked into the dining room, her father was praising the cake. Everyone was still at the table, plates pushed aside. Her mother looked up. "Who was it, Jenny?" Then she saw Rob behind Jenny. And everyone looked at them.

The moment was upon her, and Jenny said the first thing that came to mind. "Mom—everybody, this is Rob, my friend. Rob Montana." Blurted it out like that, without any preparation, and couldn't stop talking, went on swiftly, "Rob, this is my mother—"

Then Rob, hand out: "How do you do, Mrs. Pennoyer?"

And her mother, the remnants of a smile still on her face: "What did you say your name was?"

"And this is my father," Jenny said quickly, as if by introducing Rob fast enough she could leap over the reverberations of his name, "my brother Frankie, you met Ethel, and this is Mimi Holtzer."

"Hi," Rob said, carrying on. "Frankie. Mimi. Think I know your cousin, Mimi. How do you do, Mr. Pennoyer?" Again his hand was out. But Jenny's father didn't respond, looked at Rob flatly, as if he were an unwelcome salesman. "Rob *what?*"

A beat of silence passed. *They know*, Jenny thought. *They know.* "Montana," Rob said.

Mimi fidgeted with her scarf. "Montana?" She turned to Frankie. "Isn't that the same name as—"

"Montana?" Frankie had been slouched in his seat, one arm around the back of Mimi's chair. Now he pulled himself upright. His eyes darted at Rob, then Jenny.

Jenny's stomach pounded. *The name,* she thought, *the name—as if nothing else were important.*

95

"Are you related to someone named Nell Montana?" Frankie pointed a finger at Rob, and Jenny wanted to slap his hand down. "Well?" Frankie said aggressively, sounding eerily like their father.

"She's my mother," Rob said. "Nell Montana is my mother."

It was out, and everyone froze—it was almost comical. A snort of nervous laughter ran through Jenny; her eyes teared with the effort to suppress it. Her father froze in the act of lifting his coffee cup to his mouth, Frankie froze with his finger pointed, Mimi with a piece of cake in her hand, and Jenny's mother dabbing up crumbs with a napkin.

"You're—kidding!" Frankie said finally.

"No," Rob said, his voice sinking as if he'd just realized who he was and where he was and what he was up against. "I'm not kidding." In the sharpened bones of his face, Jenny saw what an effort it was for him to continue smiling. "She's my mother."

He and Jenny were still standing, while everyone else remained at the table. Abruptly, laughter gone, Jenny sat down and pushed a chair toward Rob. He sat with his back rigid, not touching the wood. Looked as if he were in the principal's office. Jenny wanted to shake him, loosen him up, uncrimp those stiff shoulders, then realized she was sitting exactly the same way.

"That's your mother?" Amelia Pennoyer said. "Your *mother*?"

"Mrs. Pennoyer, can I say someth—"

"Wait a second, wait a second, *hold on.*" Jenny's father clinked down his coffee cup. As if it were a sig-

96

nal, they were all in motion. Amelia finished brushing the crumbs, Mimi pushed back her chair, and Frankie moved closer to her, while Ethel, staring at Rob, twitched her nose like a rabbit.

Ethel's getting back at me for being so impatient with her, Jenny thought. Irrelevant, but her mind fixed on that moment with Ethel with something like relief. Ethel's anger was fixable, something she could make right. She'd talk to her later, explain she'd been nervous.

"Now, let's get this straight," Jenny's father said. "We're talking here about a woman named Nell Montana, who—" He looked at his wife and said, his voice thickening, "She was in an accident with our daughter. Is that woman your mother?"

"Mr. Pennoyer"—Rob smiled uneasily—"that's, yes, that's my mother."

"What?"

"My mother," Rob repeated.

And again they all stared disbelievingly at him. But they had known, Jenny thought, from the moment she said Rob's name. Known, but couldn't believe.

"I know how you feel," Rob began.

"The hell you do," Frank Pennoyer said. He was breathing hard. An uncharacteristic flush rose under his skin. "The *hell* you do."

"Mr. Pennoyer—it was the most terrible thing that ever happened to my mother."

Hearing Rob's words through her parents' ears, Jenny winced. How facile it sounded. *The most terrible thing. . .* As if his mother's pain could match the pain of Gail's death.

"What are you doing here?" Amelia said.

"I'm—I came to see Jenny." And again his smile, which now made Jenny want to cry out, *Don't smile.*

"Rob's here because I asked him," she said. "He's my friend. My good friend."

"Oh, my *God,*" Mimi said.

"Your good friend," Jenny's mother said, almost under her breath. She pushed back her chair and stood up.

"Mom—" Jenny began.

"No," Amelia Pennoyer said. "*No.* Don't say anything to me!" She left the room, her heels rapping on the old wooden floor. A moment later they all heard the sound of her bedroom door closing hard.

"That does it." Jenny's father put both hands flat on the table. "I don't know what you had in mind, Jenny, and I don't much care." He turned to Rob. "You leave now," he said. "You just walk yourself out of this house, pronto."

"Dad—please, can we talk?"

"There's nothing to talk about. I want him out of here."

"I think you're all narrow-minded," she burst out. "You won't even listen, give me a chance—" She had thought Frankie would stand up for her, and Mimi. Yes, surely, Mimi. Irrationally, she felt the greatest anger against Mimi. Why did she sit there with her eyes down and her hands folded so demurely in her lap!

Rob stood up. "Mr. Pennoyer," he said with dignity. "I'm really sorry I upset Mrs. Pennoyer. It was—it was nice meeting you all."

"Oh, it was *really nice* meeting you all," Jenny said into his ear as they walked into the hall.

Rob smiled lamely. "I had to say something, didn't I?"

She leaned against the wall, her arms folded. "Now wasn't that terrific? Wasn't that pleasant, though? Ugh!" She hit her hand against the wall. "It was every bit as awful as—"

"Well, next time it will be a little easier," Rob said. "At least we broke the ice."

"Next time?" She couldn't believe him. He almost looked cheerful, but she felt as if she'd taken a beating. "Didn't any of that in there get through to you?"

He squeezed her hands. "Look, Jenny, don't let them scare you. So they said *boo!* I can understand—it was a shock for them."

He bent toward her to kiss her, but she sidestepped. "Not here. Not now."

"Honey," he said sadly, and then, sorry, she held on to his jacket with both hands, silently berating herself. Why hadn't she been stronger, somehow made things clearer? The moment her mother looked at her, the moment her father raised his voice, she had felt wiped out. Her father was calling her now, and her stomach started that uneasy pounding, as if she were twelve again, instead of seventeen.

"You better go," she said to Rob. Yes, she wanted him to go, but she wanted him to stay, also. She wanted to push him out the door and wanted to leave with him.

"Jenny!" her father called again.

Rob left, and she stood at the window watching him

walk down the street. Going away from her. Why hadn't she kissed him? Why hadn't she said she loved him? Why hadn't she gone with him? She half-opened the door, then stopped. "Jenny, I'm waiting," her father called.

Rob turned the corner and disappeared. Slowly she closed the front door.

Chapter 16

"**J**enny!" Frank, Sr., called for the third time.

"Coming," she called back from the hall, but she still didn't appear. Frank's legs ached. He kneaded his calves. Maybe he should get space shoes, the ones they molded to your feet. He drew in a deep breath, let it out. The brain was a funny thing. Right there, thinking about space shoes, he'd thought, *Gail in the sky with her space shoes.*

A hollow opened up beneath his breastbone. There'd been a song Gail used to play all the time, one of those Beatles songs he couldn't understand. *Lucy in the Sky with . . . something.* Amelia had sung it to Gail when she was in the coma. They'd both sat by her bed, holding her hands, talking to her, singing, reading, the kind of thing you see in the movies. Only in the movies it would always work out. One day the beautiful girl in the coma would flutter her eyelashes, the eyes would open, and she'd . . . *smile!* And the music would rise, and even though you knew it was just a movie, you'd get this lump in your throat.

He didn't go to movies anymore. He'd rather watch TV. Anyway, he had movies going on right in his own home. What else was Jenny's bringing that Montana boy into their house but a bad movie?

"Jenny!" he bellowed. Mimi and Frankie talked in low tones, their heads close together. Frank drummed his fingers on the table, aware of his anger like some small creature rushing back and forth in his belly. Hastily, without thinking, he drank another cup of coffee. Shouldn't have done it. Now he'd be up half the night—just what he didn't need after the day he'd had.

Rough day, rough. Starting right out with Jim parking in the spot everyone knew was Frank's. From there, it had all been downhill. One thing after another. Crystal, his best cashier, out with a sick kid. Not that Crystal usually let him down. Give credit where credit was due, she had the best work record of anybody in the store, including that idiot Jim, who, the minute the weather warmed up, called in sick. Sick? He was out on the lake with his boat.

Frank should have replaced the guy years ago, but when it came to cutting meat nobody could cut the way Jim did. When you were a store manager you had to go along with people. It was like being captain of a ship. It was up to you to keep things running smoothly, keep the crew and the customers satisfied and coming back.

Half the time what you really thought you kept to yourself. Waited to see how things worked out. Like

this new girl with her la-dee-dah name. Now, who in
their right mind would name a girl Morgan? Sounded
more like a horse than a girl. She was no winner
either: skinny, big front teeth, and always gaping at
him. Today, she'd given a customer twenty dollars
too much. When she discovered it, instead of coming
to him, she'd gone hollering through the store, yelling
at the customer, "Hey, you! Hey, you!"

By the time he came home all he wanted was a
little peace and quiet. Looked like he was going to
have it, too. Good supper, Mimi over, everything
going along fine, teasing Amelia about their court-
ship, and then *bingo!* Jenny shoots it all down, brings
that boy right into their house.

His temple throbbed. He couldn't figure Jenny out.
What had she been thinking of ? Why do something
like that to her mother? Why bring everything up to
the surface again?

He had suffered over Gail. It was a hard thing to
lose a child. The hardest thing. Unnatural. Something
wrong about being alive when your kid was gone. He
had cried in his bed many nights. Amelia would have
been better off if she'd done the same thing, instead
of keeping it all to herself. She was that way, though,
and he had to respect her for it.

Maybe other women were different. He wouldn't
know. He'd lived with Amelia so many years, by now
it seemed it must have been destiny that they got
married. What was it they used to say? Kismet. *Kismet* that they had met. Funny word. Kiss met. Met
her and kissed her. He had, too. First time he'd seen
her, that day on the Erie Canal path, seen that tall

girl with brown eyes looking at him, frowning and smiling, things going across her face like clouds and sun in the sky; well, he'd just wanted her. Got her, too.

Best thing he ever did in his life. He rubbed his wet eyes. He wasn't ashamed to admit there was a sentimental part to him.

"You okay, Mr. Pennoyer?" Mimi said, looking at him anxiously.

He nodded. "Did you kids know anything about that boy?"

"No, nothing," Mimi said.

"He said he knew your cousin, Mim," Frankie said.

"I'll ask Joel. He goes to Alliance High." She sat close to Frankie.

"So you didn't know she was going to bring him here?" Frank said.

"Are you kidding, Dad? If I'd known, he wouldn't have gotten past the front door."

"Well, how was it the whole family was in the dark?" Frank said. "Doesn't your sister talk to you?"

"I'm not Jenny's keeper," Frankie said, getting his old stubborn-as-a-mule, I'm-not-giving-you-anything look.

He'd always been a hard nut to crack, Frank, Sr., thought. The fact is, if you'd asked him a year ago if his youngest son gave a fig for the family, he might have had to say he, unfortunately, didn't think so. Swear to God, nineteen years and never once had that boy looked him straight in the eye. Frank, Jr. You'd think they'd be close, but just the opposite. The truth was, to this day, when Frankie came into the room, even though they were getting along much better, Frank could feel the hairs on the back of his neck bristling.

"Where is that girl?" he said, standing up. But just then, Jenny walked in. "Sit down," he said. Then he just looked at her, trying to think where to begin, but instead remembering how a few weeks after Gail's funeral they'd all been watching TV and found themselves sitting like dummies in front of a show about a family that had lost four daughters. Four.

The father got right on TV and said, "We are the walking wounded." Must have been *60 Minutes*, maybe *PM Magazine*, one of those news shows. He'd told himself to shut it off, but before he could, Amelia had walked out looking like someone had stabbed her in the heart.

And then Jenny had turned to him and said, "Why? Why?" He'd never forget the way she said it. And even though he had the same question in his head, he'd given her an answer. "Drunken driver." As if that were the whole answer. Maybe it was. The thing was, when kids asked questions you had to answer. That's what being a father meant. You didn't let them know you had questions, too. Maybe he hadn't been the best father in the world, but he'd tried. Nobody could say he hadn't tried.

"All right, Jenny," he said a little more quietly, "let's hear it. What was the idea of bringing that boy here?"

"I told you."

"Tell me again."

She wet her lips. "Rob is my friend, and I wanted

105

you to meet him." She had her legs twisted around the rungs of the chair. Like a kid. But she wasn't a kid anymore. Seventeen. You had to be responsible for your actions at that age.

"I want a better explanation," he said.

"Dad—"

"You're off the wall, Jenny, you know that," Frankie said, interrupting. "You walk in here with this guy, out of the blue. Where's your brains? You hit Mom like a ton of bricks."

"Frankie, stay out of this," she said.

"No, I won't. That was stupid, just plain stupid. How long have you known him? How come you're friends with him? And bringing him home—that takes the cake!"

"Would you rather I sneaked around? Would you rather I gave him a false name? He's stuck with his name, okay? And he's my friend. Okay? Okay?"

"Why'd you have to pick him for a friend? Are you friends with just anybody?"

"Look, Frankie, I don't tell you not to be friends with Mimi."

"Totally different! Mimi's mother didn't—"

"No, Frankie," Mimi said, putting her hand on his arm. "That's really unfair." And then, turning to Jenny, "Jenny, try to look at it this way—"

They were all talking at once. Only Ethel said nothing, but clapped her hands over her ears.

Frank ended it. He raised his voice. "Jenny, I don't want you to see him anymore. You shouldn't have brought him here. It was selfish and thoughtless." He got to her with that. Saw her face flush, saw those long eyes fall away.

"I see him in school every day," she said.

"Don't play dumb with me, Jenny!" One thing about Jenny, he always said she had brains. Still water runs deep. To tell the truth even when she was a little tyke, he'd been sort of uneasy around her. Cute little thing, but always looking at you, looking and watching, those dark eyes, and keeping her own thoughts.

"Where's your family feeling?" he said roughly. "Where's your sense of proportion? How can you be friends with that boy?"

"Dad." She spoke quietly now. "I met Rob, and—and when I found out who he was, I knew—I tried not to—" She pressed her lips together, her face filled. He waited, didn't let her tears sway him. "We're in—" She stopped, then said, "We go together."

"Break it off," he said. "End it."

"I can't do that," she said.

"What do you mean, you can't?"

"I can't. I won't."

Frank stared at his daughter. Defiant. She gave him back one of her long, dark stares. A pain like a streak of white light passed through his eyes. He'd be lucky to get out of this without one of his headaches.

"I'm telling you again, Jenny," he said, controlling his voice. "You stop seeing that boy." He pushed away from the table, heard her say, "No, I won't," but kept moving, going to Amelia, clamping down on the anger, but all the time wondering how things like this happened.

He'd had such big dreams and plans: great kids, his own market, making a pile of money. What a laugh. Here they were in the same worn-down, shabby house they'd been in for twenty-five years. He was as far as he'd ever go, manager of the Big K Market. And as for the kids . . . When they were little, you thought you could die for them, you got this big impossible feeling in your heart. Then the years passed, and all of a sudden most of them were grown up and nothing had worked out the way you thought it would. One kid was in California, one was a mailman, one didn't give a damn for her family, and one was dead.

He turned the handle of the bedroom door. " 'Melia," he said into the darkened room, "you okay?"

Chapter 17

"**W**ell, Jenny, what are you going to do?" Her mother had come into her room while Jenny was studying and stood by the bureau in her gray-and-yellow robe, her hair in a single braid. "What have you told that boy? Are you still seeing him?"

"Mom—" Jenny had to push past the wounded look in her mother's eyes. "If you only knew Rob. He's the sort of person you'd really like. He's kind and—"

"I don't want to hear about him," her mother said in a low voice. "Surely you know that."

"You're closing your mind. It's not fair."

"Fair?" Her mother's hand was at her throat. "It seems to me that you being friends with him is more than unfair. It's a betrayal of your family. Even Mimi feels the way we do. *Family comes first.*"

"Mom, Mimi's got problems with her family, too."

"You don't have problems with your family, Jenny," her mother contradicted quietly. "Your family has problems with you." And she walked out.

The tension in the Pennoyer house since Rob's visit

had been nearly unbearable. "Just let me know when you come to your senses," her father had said, anger swelling his jaw. And then he hardly spoke to her again. His silence aroused an answering silence in Jenny. But in the middle of the night, waking with her face burning, she found herself arguing furiously. *Look, just let me lead my own life! I'm not doing this to hurt you or Mom. Why can't you understand my side of things?*

She didn't tell Rob how hard it was going for her at home. Her family hadn't exactly cut her off, but it had come down to their speaking to her only if necessary. And it wasn't only her parents who were pressing her. From California, Vince and Valerie called one night and took turns "talking sense" into Jenny.

"Interfacing with your family is a first priority," Valerie said, leaving Jenny torn between a desire to point out to her sister-in-law that *she* had hardly considered her family first when she met Vince, and an equally strong desire to laugh.

After Valerie, Vince came on the wire, playing Big Brother to the hilt. "Jenny, honey, I know how you kids take things seriously at your age. I remember, but now that I have some perspective—"

That had been enough for Jenny. She tuned out the rest of his patronizing speech. There was an unspoken agreement among all the "adults" (Frankie got included—because he was over eighteen? Or because he sided with his parents?), an agreement to refuse to believe in the depth or the validity of Jenny's feelings. That was unimportant "kid stuff."

One morning she woke up with the thought that today she was going to break through their anger, force them to talk to her, to acknowledge her right to her own friends and her own feelings.

"Good morning," she said, sitting down at the table. "Isn't it a great morning?" Her father rattled the paper. Her mother poured coffee and sat down. Pancakes were heaped on a plate in the middle of the table.

"Hi, Ethel," Jenny said.

"Hi, Jenny." Leaning on one elbow, Ethel dreamily dipped a spoon into cornflakes. Her corkscrew curls were freshly combed and held back with a pair of flowered barrettes.

"Is Frankie coming up?" Jenny said, reaching for the milk.

"I don't think so," her mother said briefly.

"Did he come in late last night?"

"Mmm."

"I had a really funny dream," she persisted. "Anybody interested in hearing it?"

"I am," Ethel said.

Jenny kept the smile on her face. "It was about cats. Someone had stolen a cat and I was yelling, 'Cat thieves! Cat thieves!' "

Ethel laughed. "Cat thieves!" she repeated.

"It wasn't funny-funny, though," Jenny said. "Actually, I woke up feeling sort of blue."

"Sometimes I have bad dreams," Ethel said. "I dream about cats, and sometimes dogs chase me in my dreams."

111

Her father cleared his throat. "Listen to this. It's from Dear Abby.

" 'How They Handle Drunk Drivers in Other Countries.' " He emphasized each word. " 'In Finland, England, and Sweden, drunk drivers are automatically jailed for approximately one year. South Africa, the drunk driver is given a ten-year prison sentence or a fine of $10,000, or both. Bulgaria, a second conviction of drunk driving is your last. The punishment is execution.' " He looked up. "They don't fool around. 'San Salvador. Drunk drivers are executed by firing squads. Malaya, the driver is jailed. If married the spouse is also jailed.' "

"Why not the children, too?" Jenny couldn't resist the remark. Her father leaned eagerly into the opening she'd given him.

"Maybe you think the penalties in those countries are too harsh? I say that it's a crime in itself that in our country people can run around in their cars committing outright murder, and get away with it. Is that your idea of justice, Jenny?"

No answer. Nothing to say. What *was* justice? Gail was dead, that was a fact. And Rob's mother was free. Another fact. Of course it wasn't justice. But would it be justice if Nell Montana were in jail?

Walking Jenny to work later that day, Rob said, "How're things on the home front?"

Jenny shrugged. "Wonderful."

"Oh, it can't be that grim. What do you think we could do to get them to accept me?"

"Nothing."

112

"Come on, Jen, there must be something."

"You really think so?"

"I do. And I think that time will make a difference, too."

"Why don't we talk about something else?" Jenny said, but before long they were drawn into the same conversation again.

"I was thinking about that day I came over," Rob said, "trying to remember—did your mother say anything? Or was it just your brother and your father?"

"Oh, she had something to say, all right."

"Where do you think I stand with your family now?"

Jenny laughed shortly. "You really want me to tell you? Pit City."

He put his arm around her waist. "Sometimes I have this really bad feeling. What if I lose you? What if they make you stop seeing me?"

"No, they can't. I'm nearly eighteen. They couldn't make me do things when I was thirteen."

"Well, you know me. I really thought things would be different. I just, somehow, didn't believe your family would be that hard-nosed."

"I warned you," she said, but in fact she, too, had let herself hope. Castles in the sky. Daydreams. Fantasies. *Rob Montana? What a splendid young man. Put it there, son. Come in, come in, welcome to the family.*

"They're your parents," he went on. "Jenny's people. Maybe I thought your mother would be a big Jenny and love me—"

"At first sight."

113

"Of course." He sighed ruefully. "I don't think I'm naïve, but I must be. I keep being surprised about people. I honestly didn't think they would be so bitter."

"They have a right to be bitter," she said. "You can see that."

"A right to be bitter," he repeated. "What does that mean? Is that like the right to vote?"

"Wow, you can be really sarcastic, Rob."

"I'm just trying to get things straight in my head, Jenny. A simple question—"

"Simpleminded!" she heard herself saying sharply. They were still walking close, but a stiffness came between them.

"I've noticed you don't like being put on the spot about your parents," he said. "You're very defensive. You jump right out of your skin every time I say anything about them."

Stop this right now, she thought. *Stop this squabbling before it turns into something bigger*. Instead she said, "I suppose you're not defensive about your mother?"

"I don't think so. I don't apologize for her—"

"Oh, come on! You do, you know you do. When you first met me you insisted she had only one drink that night. But when I met her at your house—remember this? *I* do—your mother said *two*. She said *two drinks*."

"What are you doing? You're making something out of nothing."

"Really? Two drinks appear to me to be one-

114

hundred percent more than one drink. Not what I call nothing."

"Listen, Jenny, let's leave my mother out of this. She's not working us over like your family. She's holding up her head, and it isn't easy for her."

"Ah, no, she's suffered. Isn't that what you told me?"

His arm dropped from her waist. "Now who's being sarcastic? Let me tell you something, Jenny. Let me tell you something about my mother."

"Keep your voice down. You don't have to yell."

"My mother has suffered, you're right." The bones of his face were all sharp. "You used the right word. You think what happened washed off her back? That she doesn't care? You met her and you think that? Let's be honest here. You're not everything you think you are. I know how you think about yourself, that you're so intelligent, so sensitive, but you can be just as thick and insensitive as the next person."

Her head went up like a horse's; she felt a cold calmness coming over her. It wasn't her family destroying Jenny and Rob now. They were doing it to themselves.

At the corner across from Hamburger Heaven they parted without saying good-bye.

She worked that afternoon like an automaton. "May I help you?" "Drink?" "Is this for our dining area?" And all the time their quarrel—what *she* had said, what *he* had said—sent up flares in the back of her mind, rising moments of heat, of anger, of disbe-

115

lief. They had had spats before, little to-dos over this and that. No one, least of all she, could be loving and nice at all times. They were two different people, saw the world differently, liked different things. It was good for them to spar, get their disagreements out in the open. But this was something else—this had been hurting each other.

Later that evening he called. "Hello, it's me."

She wound the cord over her arm. Her parents were in the living room. Were they listening? "Hello."

"Do you want to make up?"

"Yes. Do you?"

"I do! Look, I'm sorry for all that junk I said. I didn't mean it, you know I didn't. I was just mad—"

"We shouldn't do that to each other," she said. "We shouldn't attack each other. We don't need that."

"You looked so sad when you left."

"I was *mad*."

"You were sad, too."

"Well, you're right," she said.

"I couldn't do anything when I got home. Didn't want to study, didn't even want to eat."

"That bad?"

"I suppose you ate like a horse."

"I don't know what I ate. I don't even know what's happened since I left you. I've been on automatic. Rob, remember what we read the other day on the rock?" Someone had painted a slogan in the park. *The world's a tough place. Most of us won't come out of it*

116

alive. They had decided to adopt that as their personal motto, agreeing that there was something so crazy, funny, and true about it that, somehow, it helped put all the difficult things into perspective.

"I remember. Jenny—I love you."

"I love you, too." Were her parents listening? Well, let them. Didn't she have a right to be with Rob? To talk to him? To love him? No one asked Frankie to give up Mimi, or her father to give up her mother. Why should they tell her to give up the one she loved?

Chapter 18

"I don't go out with barefoot ladies," Rob called out of the car window as Jenny ran out of the house.

"Isn't it a perfect day?" She leaned into the open window, standing on one bare foot. "Hi! You're early." They didn't kiss, too many windows looking out on them, but rubbed their faces together. "Mmm, you smell yummy. What'd you put on your skin?"

"It's a new after-shave," he said, looking pleased.

"I haven't combed my hair yet," she said. "Otherwise, I'm about ready."

"Are you going to wear braids?"

"Okay. Do you think I should put on something fancier?" The plan was to go downtown, shop, eat lunch out, maybe see a movie. Rob, wearing dark-blue cords and a blue-and-white striped shirt, was certainly dressier than Jenny in her jeans and gray, hooded sweatshirt.

"I like the way you look," he said. "How long are you going to be?"

"Shoes, hair . . . oh, ten minutes."

He switched on the car radio, and Jenny turned to go back into the house. Halfway up the walk she turned again. "This is ridiculous, you sitting out here. You're my friend. Come on in."

Without knowing how it had happened or that it would happen, she had reached the limit of her patience. She'd had it with tiptoeing around watching what she said, and how she said it, and who she said it to. Enough already with not daring to phone Rob and whispering when he phoned her. Enough already with watching her mother's face for every little change of mood and quailing inwardly if her father's voice reached a certain pitch.

Her father had read her a Dear Abby column to break her down about Rob. Well, she could do a Dear Abby of her own.

Dear Abby,

I'm in love with a boy that my parents refuse to be civil to. Their only response to him is to tell me to give him up. Abby, he is eighteen, responsible, polite, and thoughtful. He loves me, too. This is not a teenybopper crush, Abby. We're both serious about each other and our future. We love each other tremendously, but making out is far from all we have on our minds. He's looking for work, I hold down a part-time job, we both get respectable marks in school and have plans for the future, which include college. We are not acting foolishly or immaturely. His "crime" is that he is the son of a woman who caused grief and hurt to my family. I know this has made it difficult almost beyond words for my family but, still, don't you think they should at least try to see him for himself, and to give us a chance?

Signed,
Deeply in Love

And the answer? Jenny could write that, too.

Dear in Love,
If you two are the kind of kids you describe your-selves to be, I think your parents should definitely give you a chance. Go to them and tell them Dear Abby approves.

"I don't want to make things unpleasant for you," Rob said, getting out of the car.

"I'm not suggesting any confrontations. Just Mom is home. Daddy's at work," she said as they walked toward the porch. "Frankie, too." Then, quickly, keeping her voice neutral, not wanting to hurt his pride, "Are you, er, a little worried about them? Physically, I mean?"

"Do you mean am I worried they'll beat me up?" Rob shrugged. "I thought about it the night I came over. It seemed like a real possibility."

"You didn't act scared."

"I wasn't. Not really. I don't like fights, but if you're a guy, you always half-expect somebody might take a poke at you."

"Why? What for?"

"For nothing. Just because the other guy's feeling

120

evil. It happened to me in Binghamton, and for no reason except a couple of punks didn't like the color of my eyes." He took the steps two at a time, not rushing, just moving his legs the full distance they could cover, and he was whistling under his breath, a jaunty tune between teeth and tongue.

"Do you think it's cowardly, me bringing you in when just Mom and Ethel are home? Oh, I don't care if it is! It's just the way things have worked out. We didn't plan this. Besides, Rob, I've been wondering if we didn't make a big mistake the first time, practically flinging you into everyone's faces. We might have approached it all more gradually, taken on my mother and my father separately. What do you think?"

"Are you all right?" he said.

"Yeah. I know I'm chattering. I'm nervous, I admit it, but I'll be fine. You were the one who said we had to do this, right? Have to get them used to you." She took his hand, squeezed. "How about you? How are you?"

"Ah, well, a little . . . not exactly tense, but not exactly relaxed either. Okay, actually, except for a feeling of walking into the lion's den."

The living room was empty. "Whew." Jenny rolled her eyes and they both laughed. She heard the whine of the vacuum cleaner in her mother's room. Question: Where does Rob wait in Jenny's house for Jenny?

Where would Rhoda wait? Answer: In Jenny's room, of course. "Come on." She took his hand with a great show of confidence and led the way.

The first thing he did was to go around her room and look at the pictures on the walls: Some were posters, but most were pictures she'd cut out of magazines and "framed" with colored tape. One, for instance, she had cut from an oil company ad—something about how generous, public-spirited, and philanthropic the company was—but what she had wanted was the picture used to illustrate the corny pitch: an immensely fat old woman in a shapeless lavender dress, looking into the camera with a fierce and defiant dignity. Most of Jenny's pictures were of old people. She hadn't planned it that way, had just cut out the pictures that went straight to her heart.

Next he picked up the china elephant. Then the framed picture on her bureau. "This isn't you?"

"It's Gail, when she was fourteen."

He put it down at once. "Where's your grandfather's picture?"

She pointed to the snapshot tucked into her mirror. He studied it, and she put her arms around him from behind, snugging her chin into his neck. "I'd like to have this picture of us," she said. They looked at themselves in the mirror, their faces side-by-side.

He put his hands over hers. "Let's take it."

"Cheese," they said together with big flashy grins.

"Print that one," Rob ordered. They broke apart, laughing, and she picked up her hairbrush.

Rob perched on the edge of the bottom bunk bed. "It's a funny little room, isn't it, so long and narrow? I like it."

"So do I. It used to be Frankie's." Jenny bent, her

122

hair falling over her face, and brushed vigorously. "I used to sleep in the front room with my sisters." The familiar litany slipped through her mind. *First Grandpa died, and Vince and Valerie lived in his apartment in the basement. (I was thirteen then.) Then Vince and Valerie moved to California. (I was fourteen.) Gail was killed. (I was fifteen.) And Frankie moved down to Grandpa's place. (I was sixteen.) And I moved into Frankie's room. (On my seventeenth birthday.)*

"The whole front room is Ethel's now," Jenny said, "except Gail's stuff is still there."

Again she said Gail's name with a certain deliberation. They couldn't forever avoid the painful things. It had been all right in the beginning to play the just-Rob-and-Jenny game; in fact, they really needed to do that. A way of getting over what then seemed the insurmountable hurdle of their families. And now? They weren't exactly on the other side of that hurdle, but maybe somewhere midway over it. Flying through the air and hoping not to crash, but to land on their feet.

She whipped her hair back and continued brushing. "Did that make you uncomfortable, my saying Gail's name?"

"No, you said it before—her picture. And it isn't the first time, anyway."

She nodded. "We have to talk about Gail and—everything, Rob."

"I'm willing. Only I don't want to get in fights with you. You know you get awfully tense—"

"All right, I admit it. I don't make it easy." Al-

123

ready she felt the tension of this little discussion. She sat down next to him, braiding her hair. "Was it fun playing with the band the other day?" The band director had asked him to fill in for a drummer who was out sick.

"Loved it."

"When you're a kindergarten teacher you can play the drums for your kids."

"I'm going to take piano lessons, did I tell you that?"

"No, when'd you decide?"

"I was checking out the community college catalogue again. I can take lessons and get credits toward my degree."

"Terrific."

"Yeah, I'm really glad. I think going to school here, at least for the first couple years, is going to work out. I only wish you weren't going so far away."

"Watch what you say, you may get your wish. I'm set for my first year—we got our loan—but my father says if college costs keeping going up I might have to eventually live at home and go to school around here."

"Really?" Rob brightened.

"Don't wish it on me," Jenny said. "Anyway, it's not that far away where I'm going. Only an hour's drive."

"Hour and a half. I'll come see you every weekend."

"Or I'll come see you." She handed him the rubber band for her first braid and began work on the sec-

124

ond. They were sitting that way on the bunk bed, leaning in toward each other, he winding the rubber band around her braid, she plaiting the rest of her hair, when her mother walked in. She stared at Rob, then walked out.

Chapter 19

"**Y**ou called me, Mom?" Jenny stood in the doorway of her mother's room.

"Why is he here?"

"Mom, I—" She took her mother's arm, searching for the right words. *Mom, please try to understand. Yes, Gail has been dead for two years. Yes, Rob's mother was the cause of her death. But it's been two years, Mom, more than two years, and I'm young and alive and can't stifle my feelings forever.*

"Mom, can't we—what happened is the past. Can't we forget it and—"

Her mother recoiled as if Jenny's hand were on fire. "Forget? Is that what you think, Jenny?" She rubbed her arm. "Is that what you've done? Forgotten your sister? People forget too many things, too quickly, too easily. Forget? That is the most unkind thing you've ever said to me."

A dull feeling came over Jenny. She remembered how, years ago, she and her mother had so often looked at each other without comprehension or sympathy, brown eyes meeting brown eyes, so much felt, so little said, too much misunderstood. Once, her mother had slapped her. She remembered her outrage and then her confusion as, in the moment of the slap, her mother's eyes pleaded with her for understanding.

She sighed, oppressed by the memory. Was anything ever forgotten? No, she hadn't forgotten Gail. But she blamed herself for remembering too well the bad parts: the bickering, the taunts, and fights.

"I want him to leave," her mother said. "This is my house!"

"We'll both be going in a few minutes," Jenny said.

In her room Ethel was showing Rob a picture she had drawn in school. "This is my family."

Rob looked up at Jenny. "Ethel and I are getting to know each other. She's promised to give me some piano lessons."

"Yes?" Jenny said distractedly. "Well, guess what? You're not welcome in my house."

"Look—if it's causing you trouble, I'll wait outside."

"No, don't! This is my house, also. Please!"

"Calm down, Jenny," he said quietly. "It's okay."

"You're always getting excited," Ethel said.

"Me? Are you kidding, Eth? I'm cool as a cucumber." She pushed her feet into her sneakers.

Her mother entered the room. "Here," she said, "*here.*" She thrust a yellowing newspaper clipping into Rob's hand.

"What is that?" Jenny sat down on the bunk bed. "Where did this come from?" she said, looking at the photo. "I didn't know you had this."

The picture showed a car askew in a field, its front end crumpled like paper. Nearby, a bike lay on its side with what seemed to be a large cloth on the ground next to it. In the foreground, four men, faces blurred, had been caught in purposeful mid-stride.

Underneath the picture, the caption read, "Rescue workers arrive after foreign car at left collided in the rain with bicycle in foreground. Gail Pennoyer, 16, injured in the collision, is in critical condition at the Up-state Medical Center."

"Mom, why did you keep this?" Jenny said.

"What is it?" Ethel said. "What is it? Can I see it?" No one answered her.

"Mrs. Pennoyer—" Rob began.

Jenny's mother averted her head, her hand went up as if to protect herself. "Don't say anything. I just want you to understand. You mustn't come to this house. It's not you, it's not personal, but I can't—you can't, you *mustn't*."

"All right," Rob said after a moment. "I won't come here again, Mrs. Pennoyer."

"Why not?" Ethel said. "Why won't you come here again?"

"Ethel, go and get your laundry ready," her mother said. Then to Jenny: "I want you to stop seeing him. Just stop."

Jenny didn't reply. She shoved comb, wallet, keys, and a sweater into her knapsack.

"Your sneakers are untied," her mother said.

"I want them untied. I choose to have them untied."

*   *   *

Outside she and Rob hardly looked at each other until they were in the car and pulling away from Pittmann Street. "Jen"—he reached for her hand— "that was pretty bad. God, seeing that photo—"

"Did you look at it?" she said. "I didn't want to look at it."

"I made myself. I thought it would be cowardly if I didn't."

"That was your mother's car."

"It was a little French car. They towed it to the junkyard. I think she only got a hundred bucks for it." He stopped. "I'm sorry. That was a stupid thing to say."

"Yes, it was." She sank back against the seat.

After a couple of minutes he said, "Are you mad at me?"

She brushed her hand across her forehead. "Mad? Oh, no . . ." An enormous weariness had seized her. Her arms and legs were leaden. "Right now, I don't know how I feel," she said. But in fact, she felt so much she could hardly hold it all inside. Seeing the picture of the death car and Gail's bicycle had hit her hard.

She watched the passing streets.

Gradually she noticed that daffodils were in bloom everywhere, wonderful clumps of gold in even the smallest, meanest yards. Her spirits rose in rebellion against the leaden, deathly feeling that had her by the throat. She had held so much back with her mother. She had held her tongue, held her words, choked on her feelings to avoid a fight, to avoid hurting her mother. But how futile! Wasn't it clear that as long as she continued to see Rob she couldn't avoid hurting her mother?

Rob kept glancing at her. "I'm okay," she said. "I'm getting okay. Give me time."

He put his arm around her, drove with one hand.

"I'll tell you what," she said presently, "I refuse to be depressed. Let's do everything we said we would. Have fun shopping, eat lunch at a really nice place, and then a movie later." She bent over and tied her sneaker laces.

"I want them that way," Rob mimicked. "I *want* them untied."

Jenny raised her eyebrows. "For your information, untied shoelaces—as Mrs. Tedesco would say—are undoubtedly symbolic. Highly symbolic," she said in Mrs. Tedesco's nasal chirp. "And if you can't *relate* to that *obvious* fact—"

Rob laughed obligingly. They were both working at being cheerful. In the mall they bought tee shirts for Rob and socks for Jenny, then took the escalator up to The Happy House, where they compared tastes in dishes, linen, and crystal.

"Everything is so bloody expensive," Jenny said. "I don't see how people afford anything."

"If we started buying stuff now . . ." Rob said.

"A hope chest?" What would she put in a hope chest? Wishes and what-ifs instead of linens and towels? Not wanting to, she thought again of the picture her mother had kept, that scene she had only imagined: Gail's bike twisted, the car in the field. Rob's mother might have been sitting inside the car when the picture was taken, stunned, shocked into sobriety. Or maybe the police had already come, already taken her away. Had she spent the night in jail?

As they got off the escalator on the first floor, Rob said, "Look where we landed." They were outside The Candy Consortium. "Let's get us some jellybeans."

"They stick in your teeth."

"But they're pretty."

"Chocolate tastes better."

"Jellybeans last longer."

"Yes?" the woman behind the counter said. "You want something?" Like the walls, she was all in white, a candy nurse.

"We haven't made up our minds yet," Jenny said.

"If you really want chocolate, we'll get it," Rob said.

"No, no, jellybeans are fine."

"We'll have a quarter pound of chocolate," he said to the clerk.

"Make that jellybeans, please," Jenny said.

"Which one?" she asked.

"Jellybeans," Jenny said.

"Chocolate," Rob said.

The clerk snorted. Rob and Jenny looked at each other and snickered, and Jenny realized that without even trying they were having a good time together. But at almost the same moment her mind clicked out her mother's words. *I want you to stop seeing him. Just stop.*

* * *

She came home to a darkened house, her mother in her room. "Mom's got a headache," Ethel said. She had set the table. "You're supposed to make supper. I'm hungry."

"So why didn't you eat? You're big enough to make yourself some food."

"I'm not supposed to eat between meals."

"Oh, Eth!" Such a sober little citizen. "Break the rules once in a while," Jenny said, giving her a piece of bread and jam.

She went to her mother's room and tapped lightly on the door. The room was dark, her mother in bed with a white cloth across her forehead. "Mom? Can I get you something?"

"Go away, Jenny," her mother said. "You were with him all day, weren't you?"

A muscle twitched in Jenny's cheek. "Yes."

Her mother lifted her head, holding the cloth with one hand. "I showed you the picture," she said. "I showed you the picture! I thought you'd understand."

Jenny sagged against the door. *I do understand. Believe it or not, I know how you feel. You don't like Rob because of whose son he is. But why can't you understand that I love him? Doesn't that count for anything? Why can't you understand how I feel?*

"You're young. I don't want to hurt you." Her mother spoke in such a low voice that Jenny strained to hear her. "I've tried, I've really tried. I tell myself: Amelia, leave her alone. She's young. Don't think about it. I tell myself that, and then I wake up in the middle of the night and I think about Gail. And I

132

think about his mother, and I can't stand it. I can't stand it that you're with him. It's as if Gail doesn't matter anymore." She rolled over onto her side, her back to Jenny.

Jenny stood helplessly, her eyes stinging. All afternoon she and Rob had giggled relentlessly as if saying to each other, *Look what a good time we're having!* They had gone to a movie; she hardly remembered any of it, the title was something like *Wreck* or *Salvage*, only that there had been innumerable scenes of car chases: speeding cars leaping over police barriers, hurtling over bridges, and smashing into concrete abutments and brick walls. When they emerged into the light her head throbbed, she felt disembodied, and her ears were numb from the sounds of screeching metal and exploding cars.

After a moment, when her mother didn't say anything else, Jenny went back to the kitchen. Automatically she opened a can of mushroom soup, boiled potatoes, and tore up lettuce for a salad. Her father wouldn't be home until around ten o'clock, and Frankie was out, so it was just her and Ethel.

She poured milk for Ethel and sat down with her. Ethel mashed her potatoes with a fork and her hand. "Pass me the butter, Jenny. We went to the fire station yesterday. It was a field trip."

"That's nice." Jenny stirred her spoon around in the soup plate.

Ethel ate fast, drank her soup, and finished her milk. "They let us go up on the fire engines. They let us go upstairs where they sleep. Someone almost fell down the hole with the pole in it."

"That's nice." The movie kept coming back to her. Stupid movie! Why had they continued to sit through it? They should have walked out. People had screamed in the theater. She had screamed once, too. She felt that same scream rising in her throat. *I should break up with Rob.* The thought sent her out of her chair. She spilled her soup into the sink and filled a bowl with strawberry ice cream for Ethel. "You want marshmallow gunk on it?" There was a painful dryness in her eyes. *It's no good. Stop seeing him. You're hurting Mom too much.* She set the bowl of ice cream in front of Ethel.

"Don't you want some?" Ethel's voice was subdued. Jenny shook her head. "Are you sick, too?"

"No."

"Why aren't you talking to me then? You said it was good somebody almost fell down the hole in the fire station."

"I did? I must have been . . . Ethel, I'm sorry. I'm—thinking." Was that what she was doing? Thinking? Or was it feeling, reacting, admitting something she had been denying for weeks? Admitting that she was paying too high a price—making others pay too high a price—for her happiness?

Later she gave Ethel a warm bath, scrubbing her with a loofah and then doing finger plays with her. "Eeencie weencie spider went up the water spout," they sang together, twisting their hands into the air. "Down came the *rain* and washed the spider *out* . . ."

134

Chapter 20

"**Y**ou have reached a disconnected number," a nasal, recorded voice informed Jenny. "Please check with your operator."

Jenny dialed again, her fingers large and clumsy. This time Rob's mother answered. "Montanas'."

She could still hang up. Wait till tomorrow. Say what had to be said when she saw him in school. Wasn't it cowardly to do things this way? Hit and run on the phone. *Hello, Rob. Me, Jenny. It's all over now, we're not going to see each other anymore.* Then put down the phone, go to her room, and never come out again.

"Hello? Hello—"

"May I speak to Rob?"

"Who's calling?"

"Ah, Frances," Jenny improvised, not wanting to get into a conversation with his mother. But how stupid. What difference did it make now?

"Just a moment, Frances. Rob? Telephone, honey, it's Frances."

"Who?" she heard him yell.

"Frances. Come on." She sounded weary.

A moment later Rob came on, gave a puzzled hello.

"Hello," Jenny said, "it's me."

"It's you?"

"Yes—Frances."

"Frances! I'd know your voice anywhere, Frances. Well. This is a treat, a real treat. Do you know this is the first time in ages you've called me?"

"I know."

"And here I thought you had trouble remembering my phone number, Frances."

His joviality alarmed her. She had somthing serious, awful, to say to him. But how to begin? Where? With what? Had there been a moment she could fix on? A single moment when it had come to her that her mother, her father, Frankie—all of them—had been right? That all along she had been self-absorbed, had thought only of herself: *her* feelings, *her* pleasure, *her* life. The truth had come on her in a series of small shocks. It wasn't her mother's headache, it wasn't the picture of the mangled bike, nor was it her father's angry reading of the Dear Abby column. It was none of these things alone, but all of them added together.

"How are you?" Rob said. "To what do I owe the great pleasure of this rare phone call, Frances?"

"I—just—I have to talk to you—"

"Your voice sounds funny."

"Yes . . . I—" Was he receiving her message? *Rob, we can't go on. We're not going to see each other again.* Perhaps it would all happen soundlessly. He

136

would know, simply know . . . and hang up. And that would be the end.

"Are you getting a cold or something?" he said

"No." *Rob, no more. No more us.*

"You sound so funny," he said again. "Did something happen?"

A scene from the movie yesterday came back to her: a green car rushing headlong toward destruction. The filmmakers had photographed it so that the car seemed to be hurtling off the screen straight into the audience. Involuntarily she had screamed and clutched Rob's arm. Now she felt that same uncontrollable jolt in her stomach, the scream in the back of her throat.

"I don't want to talk anymore," she said abruptly. "I'll see you tomorrow."

"Wait! What's the matter? I know something—"

"I can't talk. I can't talk right now."

"Do you want me to come over?"

"No." She almost hated him for making this so difficult. Wasn't he supposed to be tuned into her wavelength? Hadn't they talked about ESP and the times they'd thought of the very same things at the very same moment? Where was all that inner understanding, that unspoken communication now? But most of all she hated herself for being a coward. *Say it.* But she couldn't squeeze the words out of her rigid throat.

After she hung up she walked up Jericho Hill, over to the park, and through all the familiar streets, until it was dark and she was tired; then she went home.

She told him the next day at noon. She said it immediately and briefly. "I'm not going to see you anymore." She was very cold and seemed to have no emotions.

"I don't believe you," he said. He was even smiling.

She said it again. "I'm not going to see you anymore. I can't do this to my family." He just looked at her. She gave him back the white china elephant with pink feet. Then he believed her.

Chapter 21

"*O*kay, girls, you ready for us?" A group of men from the contruction site across the street, all wearing yellow hard hats, were in Hamburger Heaven.

The rush had started. Women from the rope factory, high school kids, mothers, and children, all the hungry mouths waiting to be fed.

"Thank you, come again, and have a nice day." Jenny pushed a tray full of food toward two girls. "Yes. May I help you?" she said automatically to the next person, looked up, and it was Rob. Instantly her throat dried out, her heart pounded, her palms got sweaty. *All the classic symptoms*, she thought.

"Did you mean it?" he said.

She nodded, stiff-necked, a hard, tight gesture.

"You're breaking us up?"

Another nod.

"Would you mind telling me why?"

"I told you, Rob—"

"Tell me again." He leaned toward her, smiling.

No, not a smile, though his teeth showed. His face tightened as his lips drew back, making him look almost wolfish, fierce. An expression she had never seen.

Awful Albert was looking her way. There was a line behind Rob. "I'm not supposed to talk to customers," she said. "Do you want something?"

"I want an explanation."

Awful loomed nearby. "Problem, Jenny?"

"I'll have a hamburger and lime soda," Rob said.

"Hamburger," Jenny ordered into the mike. She drew the soda, and Albert passed on into the kitchen.

"You okay?" Phyllis jostled past her.

"Cover for me for a few minutes, Phyl." Jenny moved to one side of the counter. Rob followed. They stared at each other.

"Jenny—" He sounded bleak. "Have you really thought about this?"

"Of course I have!"

Rob's hamburger was passed through the window in its little sealed bag. She set it in front of him. He pushed it away. "Will you change your mind?"

"I can't."

"I won't ask you again."

"No," she said, as if agreeing with him. She remembered how he'd persisted after they had first met: how he'd come to meet her after work, called her on the phone, not given up even when she had given him no encouragement. And she remembered, too, how glad she'd been that he was determined, that it was his determination which had finally overcome her

140

scruples, her fear that no good could come of their friendship. Well, after all, she had been right.

"Rob—" She leaned toward him. "I just can't. It's the way it has to be."

"The way it has to be," he repeated ironically. "All right. Fine." The wolfish grin reappeared. "That's fine, then."

"I'll have a fishburger," a man in a knit cap said. "Double fries, vanilla thick shake, large." Automatically she took out her pad. She called the order in, rang up the bill, made change, and folded down the tab on the soda carton. "Thank you. Have a nice day. Come see us again."

"Doesn't this make you nostalgic?" Rhoda linked arms with Jenny. They had met at the corner of Jericho Hill and Hazard Street, their old meeting place. "Sometimes it seems like we had the best times when we were thirteen. I was maybe a little dumb when I was thirteen, but at least I didn't feel confused all the time. It's funny—Mom and Dad and I went out to supper the other night and they were fussing over me—the usual. 'Rhoda, sit up. Rhoda, use your napkin. Rhoda, there's ketchup on your cheek.' They don't exactly nag, but you know—"

Jenny smiled briefly. "I know."

"Well, and then I remembered another time we were out to dinner, years ago. They were doing their number on me and I looked over at another family where nobody was saying *anything*. It was parents and a couple of kids, and they were all just sitting at

141

the table, shoveling in the food and not talking. And I thought, Oh, those *poor kids!* I can just remember how smug I felt that my parents loved me so much. And now—" She sighed and squeezed Jenny's arm. "Last night when they started the Rhoda-sit-up stuff, I wanted to smash something. I wanted to smash them." Her arm tightened on Jenny's, she walked faster. "You don't know how guilty it makes me feel to even say it. I wouldn't say it to anyone but you."

"Rhoda—I broke up with Rob."

"What?" Rhoda stopped walking.

"I told him the other day."

"Why?"

"It has to do with my family. Like you. Only different. I was hurting my family, being selfish. Thinking just about myself. You know how they feel about me and Rob."

They walked in silence for a few moments, then Rhoda said, "Don't take this wrong, Jen, but at least *something* has happened to you."

"Rhoda, don't—"

"No, I mean it. You had a love affair and now it's over, and you're suffering. I don't want to sound callous, but all the same it's like something out of a novel. It's like Romeo and Juliet, and did you ever notice, Jen, your first initials and theirs—"

"Yes," Jenny said tensely, "and it doesn't mean a thing. I used to cry over books, but they're just books. When it happens to you— Look, you don't know what you're saying. You're talking about something you don't know anything about."

"You don't have to sound so damned superior."

"I don't feel superior, Rhoda. You don't *know*. You haven't been in love. So what if something has happened to me? It hurts!"

They walked the rest of the way to school in silence.

The break was made and Jenny didn't want to see Rob. What she had said to Rhoda was only too true. She was hurting. She told herself to avoid Rob by any means, but this wasn't entirely in her control. That week she saw him several times in the corridors.

Each time he looked her full in the face. With love? scorn? anger? hatred? "It's over," she told herself repeatedly. "It's over."

As if to prove it, she told her mother, "I've broken up with Rob." Her mother was at the piano, Jenny passing through the living room. She tossed out the words hurriedly.

"What?" Her mother looked up. "What did you say, Jenny?"

She was forced to say it again. "I've broken up with Rob."

"You've done it?" her mother said. "Oh, Jenny, that's good."

And later her father came to her, put his hand on her shoulder and said, "Jenny, your mother told me. I'm glad you came to your senses."

Not exactly hosannahs, but what did she want? Waltzes and trumpets and applause? Did she want them to beat their heads in gratitude? To cry out their praise? The fact was they were pleased and relieved.

Still, she had not at all "come to her senses." She

143

realized this the day she came of the chem lab and saw Rob walking down the hall with another girl. In a single, swift, furious glance Jenny saw that the other girl was dark-and-honey pretty with armfuls of silver bracelets and a dazzling white smile. Rob's eyes met Jenny's, and there was a moment, a fraction of a moment, when something gleamed between them, something private and only for her. Then he turned back to the girl and said something to make her smile. Jenny walked steadily toward the two of them, past them, and into her next class.

And only then, for the first time, did she fully understand what she had done. She had sent Rob away. She had cut the line between them. With a handful of words she had ended something that was beyond words, beyond either words or silence, something that no one could see but which, nevertheless, was real. They had made their love together. She alone had destroyed it.

Chapter 22

Over the weekend Rhoda gave a party. "What's the occasion?" Jenny asked.

"Nothing special, I just want to give a party. It's May, and I feel like having a party. And I want you there."

"I don't know, Rho, I don't feel very partyish."

"Come on," Rhoda said, "you can't gloom around forever. Just show up for a couple hours."

Once committed, Jenny went all the way and wore a long, multicolored skirt, a pale yellow blouse, and strings of beads. "Good," Rhoda said, turning Jenny around to inspect her costume. "Come say hello to Ma."

Mrs. Rivers patted Jenny's hand, exclaimed over her blouse, and said, "Jenny Pennoyer, how you've grown," as if Jenny were still thirteen years old.

Rhoda snorted. "Ma! Cut it out."

The party was downstairs in the game room. Rhoda's loyal troop was there, of course, and a lot of other kids. Jenny knew most of them. Nick Christopher came over to her almost immediately and asked if she wanted to dance. "Yes." She danced, was glad she'd come.

"Have you picked out your college?" she asked Nick when the music stopped. A big, husky boy, he was known in school as a science genius.

"MIT."

"Not Harvard?"

"I didn't even apply. I've always wanted to go to MIT."

It was close in the room. Someone dropped a glass, someone else screamed with laughter. "Having a good time?" Rhoda asked, passing by with bags of chips. She winked. "See?" she said.

"What was that about?" Nick asked.

"Oh, I almost didn't come."

"I'm glad you did." He had long plumes of dark, extravagantly wavy hair. Very good-looking guy. Something stirred pleasantly in her belly. "Hot in here, isn't it?" he said. "Want to step outside?"

In the Rivers' backyard they leaned against the house. TV antennas, like elaborate crosses, filled the gray night. Nick lit a cigarette. "Do you smoke? No? I have a habit already. Pack a day. I should give it up before I really get hooked." He smoked with his elbow cupped in the palm of one hand.

Leaning against the house, Jenny allowed a slow, drifting ease to come over her. For the first time in weeks, she was not concentrated like a point of blazing light on Rob.

146

"You're a good friend of Rhoda's, aren't you?" Nick asked.

Jenny smiled. Next would come a plea for her to put in a word with Rhoda on his behalf. "We've been friends for ages."

"How come you're never around when we all get together?"

"You mean the harem?"

Nick laughed. He had a bit of a giggle. "Who calls us that?"

"Sorry, that's my private— Hope I didn't offend you."

He tapped ash into his palm. "The harem!" He laughed again. "Rhoda says you broke up with your boyfriend." She nodded. "So, look—" He dropped his cigarette and put his hand lightly on her face. "How about us?"

His hand was warm on her skin. "Us?" All at once she wanted—needed, really—to be held, to be close. She leaned toward him; he put his arms around her. How good it was to lean, to let go, to feel the knot she had been tied into loosening. She put her arms around him, tucked her face into his neck. As she had done with Rob. He drew her closer. Not the way Rob hugged, not the way Rob smelled, not Rob's skin, or the sound of his voice. All she could think was, *Oh, Rob, why isn't this you?*

Nick bend toward her; they kissed, but her lips were unresponsive. She let him kiss her, didn't kiss back, couldn't kiss back. He knew. Of course he knew. He was no dope.

"Jenny?"

"I'm sorry, Nick." She would love him if she could. It seemed unfair that she couldn't love Nick. He was nice, so nice, and she was ready to love him; she would *welcome* loving him if it meant a way of forgetting Rob. "It's not you. It's just— It's too soon."

He looked at her thoughtfully. "Your boyfriend? You still have it bad? I know about it, Jenny. I broke up with a girl last year and it wasted me for weeks." He linked hands with her. "When you're ready, when you're feeling better, let me know. Okay?"

"You *are* nice," she said.

"I have a surprise for you," her father said at supper on Sunday night. "Can you guess?"

"Three guesses," Ethel said.

"Animal, vegetable, or mineral?" Jenny asked.

"Something you want," her mother put in.

"Tell me what it is," Ethel urged. "Whisper in my ear, I won't tell." Her mother whispered, and the child cried out, "The car! Daddy fixed the car!"

"Finished it this afternoon." Her father tossed Jenny the keys.

"Wow. Well, I don't know what to say."

"Why don't you take it right out for a spin, see how it rides?"

She backed carefully out of the driveway. Her parents came out on the porch to watch. She waved, sat straight behind the wheel, and glided smoothly down the street. It really was wonderful of her father to have put in all that work and time. The car had been

148

half a junk heap when he'd spotted it in a used car lot. As she drove, her pleasure increased. This was her car, she had almost paid it all off, and a great sense of anticipation and freedom came over her. She drove through the city and out to Blue Lake Park.

Turning on the dims, she drove slowly through the long road that wound through the park. A mistake. She began to feel sad. On the way home she kept passing places where she and Rob had been together. *That's the diner we went into that time with Carl. Didn't we buy sodas in that drugstore one day? Oh! There's the tree we leaned against . . . hugging . . . it was raining.* The hug she remembered especially. How they had held and held each other, just held each other without speaking.

A week. Another week. Still she came out of work looking for Rob, forgetting that she had no right and no reason to look for him. She went on dreaming about him. And absently writing his name in her notebook and then, seeing what she had done, inking it out.

One day she saw him downtown, dawdling under a big yellow umbrella with that same girl. Jenny knew who the girl was now: Suzi Slayton. She was a sophomore, on the cross-country team, and vice-president of her class. She was pretty, had an adorable figure, and was considered a VIP.

How quickly, how easily Rob had found someone else. All his talk about love, and forever, and how they were meant for each other, and how close they were, and what had any of it meant?

149

The following Saturday she took her AP math exam, forgetting that he would be taking it, too. As soon as she walked into the big room she saw him. She sat as far from him as she could get. He turned his head slightly and seemed to glance past her shoulder. He was wearing a blue shirt the color of his eyes.

Rhoda came in, sat next to Jenny. She had paper clips dangling from her earlobes. "Did I see you driving downtown yesterday?"

"Possibly." Casual voice, conscious of Rob ahead of her.

"I yelled, but you didn't hear." She bent toward Jenny. "You see who else is here?"

The exam came. From the corner of her eye she saw him bent over his paper. What if he spoke to her when the exam was over? She stared at a problem.

Hello, Jenny. (Soft)

Hello, Rob. (Calm)

I've missed you. (Intensely)

I've missed you, too. (Quietly)

Won't you reconsider, Jenny? (Pleading)

I've thought of it, but— (Calm)

But what? (Hoarsely)

Nothing's changed for me. And you have a new friend. (Dignified)

They finished the exam at almost the same time. She walked out of school a step behind him. Suzi was waiting for him. Pink lips, blue overalls. Same blue as Rob's shirt—on purpose? It was raining again. The yellow umbrella went up. Jenny walked toward the east side, near the railroad tracks. The sky was clouded, dark. The whole month had been nothing but rain. Cars passed, headlights on. Her feet were wet. She lost track of time, kept trying to outwalk the turmoil in head and belly. Why did she feel everything in her stomach? Everyone always talked about the heart, but her feelings seemed to rise directly from her stomach.

A toe on her left foot throbbed. What was she doing? Getting soaked. Stupid. Meaningless. That was the way everything seemed to her just then: senseless and without meaning.

Chapter 23

"I want to leave my sneakers here," Jenny said, stopping in front of The Sole Survivor.

"Fine," her mother said, "I'll run over to Nicholes, see if I can find that can opener."

A young man, dark-eyed, sat at a sewing machine. "Yes? Hello?"

"I'd like these sneakers resoled, please." Jenny put her packages down on the counter.

"Customer," the young man called, and Nell Montana came out from behind a curtain. She was wearing a shirt that looked vaguely Indian and had big silver hoops in her ears and silver and turquoise jewelry around her neck.

"May I help you?" she said, then recognized Jenny. "Jenny?"

"How are you, Mrs. Montana?"

"Oh, just—I'm . . ." The sentence trailed off. Although dressed gaily, Nell Montana didn't look good: a lack of color, her eyes unhealthily dark. She took the sneakers and handed Jenny a ticket. "Rob told me about you two," she said. "You made him very unhappy. He didn't want to tell me, he didn't want to upset me, but I knew something was wrong. I got it out of him."

Jenny twisted the ticket in her hand. Behind her, she heard her mother. "Ready, Jenny?"

"Yes, I'm coming!" She grabbed her packages, but then her mother was there, and Nell Montana was saying, "Your mother?" And to Amelia, "You're Jenny's mother?"

"Yes," Amelia said pleasantly.

"You're Mrs. Pennoyer? I've wanted to meet you." She reached for Amelia's hand. "Oh, how I've wanted to meet you. I'm Nell Montana."

Jenny's mother drew in a sharp breath. "You're—"

"Yes."

"Please. Let go of me."

"Hear me out—"

"I don't want—"

"Hear me *out*. I need to talk to you. I have needed to talk to you for a long time."

Jenny stood frozen. Behind them the sewing machine whirred. The man looked up and smiled uncomprehendingly as if the two women, their heads so close, their hands joined, were having a social chat.

"Do you know that I can't sleep?" Nell Montana leaned farther over the counter, her words tumbling out. "I used to go to bed at night and before I fell asleep I'd make up stories about things that were going to happen. Great things—for my son, my daughter, even me. I had silly dreams I'd be discovered, become famous, maybe a model, a country singer. I'd dream like that and fall asleep smiling, that was the sort of person I was. Then I went out one night . . ." Her voice faltered.

"Jenny, we have to go," her mother said, but Nell Montana didn't relinquish her grip.

". . . and there was a party and it was raining and—and everything changed. I—oh, what *happened* was, it was—I couldn't stop crying! No. And my whole life . . . nothing since then . . . nothing . . . it's all changed, changed. Do you understand?" The dark, sunken eyes glowed feverishly.

Amelia's lips were pressed together, splotches of color flushed her cheeks and forehead.

"I tell you, you must forgive me. I need that. I need your forgiveness. I am living in hell." She said this quietly, as if exhausted.

"Not a day goes by," she went on, "not a day, I swear to you, not a single day . . . I know. I know how you feel. You think I'm heartless. I read your letter. You think I don't know. But I have a daughter, too. I know. I know how you feel."

"No," Jenny's mother said, the color mounting and mounting in her face. She wrenched her arm free. "You still have your daughter. My daughter is gone." She ran out of the store.

"Come back," Nell Montana cried. "Come back!"

The man at the sewing machine looked up. "You called?"

Nell Montana walked past him into the back room

and Jenny, heartsick, gathered up the packages and went after her mother.

In the car, going home, her mother wept. "What does she want of me? What should I have done?"

Driving, Jenny reached out, touched her mother's knee. "Mom . . ." But she didn't know what to say. She herself was overwhelmed by confusion. Who was right? Who was wrong?

Her mother pressed her face to the window. "I couldn't forgive her. I can't. In my heart, I don't forgive her."

Chapter 24

LOCAL WOMAN HOSPITALIZED OVERDOSE SLEEPING PILLS

Nell Montana, 38, of 45 East Street, late last night was taken to Community Hospital after, police say, her son, Robin Montana, 18, of the same address, found her unconscious in her bed. An empty bottle of prescription sleeping medication was allegedly found next to her. Her condition was described by hospital authorities as guarded. Her son denied that it was a suicide attempt. "Mom had trouble sleeping some nights," he said. "Maybe she woke up and forgot she'd already taken her sleeping pills."

The woman at the semicircular desk in the hospital lobby flipped cards. People hurried past carrying suitcases and pots of flowers. The rows of red plastic chairs were filled with other people reading, smoking, talking. It was like a hotel lobby, Jenny thought. Phone booths, a gift shop, a newspaper and candy stand, a florist shop, and all the "guests" bustling around. Only the occasional white-uniformed figure and a certain antiseptic smell testified openly to its true function.

"Four-fifteen," the receptionist said. "Elevator to your right."

On the fourth floor the nurses' station was empty. Following the numbers painted on the walls, Jenny found 415 and entered. Two beds, one empty. Nell Montana asleep in the bed next to the window. A breeze blew in, stirring the gaily patterned blue-and-ivory curtains. Jenny looked down at the woman's white, white face. There were thin plastic tubes in her nose and a tube taped to the back of her hand leading to a glass jar of clear solution.

Only yesterday Nell Montana had worn an embroidered Indian blouse and there had been silver in her ears. Now she lay helpless. Punished at last, even if by her own hand? Were things finally even? Gail dead, Nell Montana almost dead.

Looking down at the woman who had killed her sister, Jenny tasted unexpected iron in her mouth. *You blundered, Mrs. Montana. Almost isn't good enough. What good is an almost death? An eye for an eye, remember? A death for a death.*

She gripped the bed railing. So inside her there lived the same raw emotions that were so near the surface with her mother! Anger and the urge to hurt and give pain in return for pain. Nell Montana stirred, and a trickle of saliva slipped down the side of her mouth. The wave of atavistic feeling drained from Jenny, and she thought of Rob. His mother had done this, not just to herself, but to him, too.

Then pity overwhelmed her. Pity for Rob, pity for the white, frail figure in the bed. She drew in a deep breath, dizzy with the rush of conflicting emotions. She bent close to the sleeping woman, studying her. A sigh escaped her. *No, I don't hate you, Mrs. Montana. I don't want you dead. You did something awful, but you're Rob's mother. How can I hate you? Even if you were somebody else—you're not the sort of person I'd hate. You killed my sister, though! I don't think I can ever forget that. Should I? No, Mom's right—there are some things you shouldn't forget. Still . . . if you wanted my forgiveness, not my mother's, I'd—I'd give it to you.*

Walking back to the elevator, down the corridor, she saw Rob coming toward her. She had half-expected this, half-feared it, but she was still unprepared. He saw her, seemed to hesitate, then nodded.

"I read about your mother in the paper," she said.

"They put it in?"

"This morning. It said you found her."

"Yes, when I came home from work."

"I didn't know you were working."

"Slayton's Garage," he said, "over on Tompkins Avenue."

"Oh. When did she—your mother—how long was

158

she unconscious?" All the time aware, so aware of his nearness.

"They figure I found her about an hour after. I wasn't even going to come right home," he said explosively. "When I think—there was a movie I wanted to see—but I felt greasy, wanted a shower. If I hadn't—"

"But you did," Jenny said. "You did find her in time, Rob." She wanted desperately to touch him, his hair, his face. "There was nobody at the nurses' station, so I just went ahead into her room. I hope that's okay? She was sleeping the whole time." She hesitated, wondering if she should tell him about their mothers' meeting in the shoe shop. "Is she going to be all right?"

He nodded.

"I'm glad. When she wakes up, will you tell her I was here?"

"I'll do that, Jenny."

A bell rang. A knot of people waited in front of the white elevator doors. "You must have—didn't you go to school today?" he said.

"I left after first period." Was he remembering another day when they had skipped school together? The elevator doors slid open.

"It was good of you to come," he said formally.

"Please let me know if I can do anything," she said, equally formally. Then the doors closed.

Later, at home, she found the morning newspaper where it had been piled on the back porch and tore out the article about Rob's mother. She folded it and put it in her desk drawer. Then she took Gail's picture and kissed it. "Oh, Gail," she said, wondering if there was ever to be an ending to what had been started that afternoon more than two years ago, when she and Gail had had one of their silly spats.

Chapter 25

"**Y**our car!" someone said behind Jenny as she unlocked the Dart in the school parking lot.

"Right," she said, turning. It was Rob, a green baseball cap tipped up on his mass of curls.

"Your father finally finished working on it."

"I know, isn't it amazing? It's terrifically peppy; you can just zoom around other cars." She dropped her books in the front seat. It was a hot, windless day. The smell of tar rose from the parking lot. So they were talking again, she thought, shading her eyes from the sun. She had wondered if those moments in the hospital were to be repeated, or if that break in the ice had been a one-time thing.

He looked at her, then away. He didn't seem as tired as the other day in the hospital. In fact, he looked wonderful wearing a tight blue tee shirt.

"How long have you had the car?"

"A little over a week," she said, thinking of all the small daily things they didn't know about each other anymore. "How's your mother? I called the hospital yesterday, and they said she was fine, but you know how that is—just a switchboard. Whoever answered sounded totally out of it."

"No, she's—well, not fine," he said, "but much better. She's coming home today."

"So soon? That's wonderful. When I saw her, I thought—" Jenny broke off, didn't want to say that Nell Montana had looked on the far side of life. "She was so white—"

"I know, I thought she'd have to be in longer, too." The sun beat down, turning his head into a halo. On his arm the little golden hairs caught the light.

"She told me she saw your mother," he said.

Jenny blinked. "Pardon?"

"My mother said she met your mother in the mall. Did you know?"

Jenny hesitated, then said, "I was there."

"I didn't know that. You heard them talking? What did they say? What happened?"

"Didn't she tell you?" On the playing field beyond the parking lot the girls' softball team was doing push-ups. "And a one and a two," the coach yelled. "Come on, Kim, and a five and a . . ."

"Just that she met your mother and that it upset her."

Jenny bit her lip. A door slammed, someone shouted for Randi, and a car packed with kids backed out next to them, the horn blowing all the way to the street. "I'm not sure if I should tell you." She slid into the car and looked out the window at him. "I

162

don't mean that the way it sounds. Just—"

He came around the other side and got in the car next to her. "Did what they talked about have anything to do with what my mom did? With taking the pills?"

"How would I know, Rob?" she said.

"You know what she does every night, Jenny? In case she can't sleep she takes two of those little white pills and puts them on her night table, and then she closes the bottle and puts *that* on her bureau. So if she wakes up in the middle of the night and those two pills are gone, she *knows* she's taken them, and won't take any more by mistake. Does that sound like a person who would take an accidental overdose?"

Jenny pressed her hands to her eyes. After a moment she said, "Look, I went into The Sole Survivor to leave my sneakers, and then my mother came in, and your mother said to her, 'I'm Nell Montana,' and they talked—no, that's not right. They didn't talk so much as your mother told my mother about herself and that she wanted her to forgive her for—you know, for Gail. And my mother—"

"Your mother what? Your mother wouldn't?"

"Rob, she was terribly upset."

"What kind of person is she?" he said. "I'm really curious. Does she know what she did to my mother? I thought when I met her she was a kind person, even though—"

"She didn't do anything to your mother, Rob. That's really unfair. Your mother did it to herself. You just said so."

163

"It seems to me she had a little help. And not from her friends."

"You don't know," she exclaimed. "You don't know at all. My mother cried. She cried when she left your mother."

"I'm terribly impressed."

"I never knew you could be so nasty," she said quietly.

"You didn't stick around long enough to learn much of anything about me."

They glared at each other. He took a pack of cigarettes out of his pants and punched in the cigarette lighter. "I didn't know you smoked," she said coldly.

"Now you do." She didn't tell him the cigarette lighter didn't work.

She had always been afraid they would fight over their parents, that the grief and anger of their parents would come between them. Well, now it had, but it didn't signify, didn't matter, because in truth nothing could come between them anymore. They were no longer a unit, a pair. They were split, they were apart, they were separate. And nothing touched, not their heads, not their hearts.

"You should have told me about their meeting," he said accusingly. "Where the devil is that lighter?" He punched it again. "Under the circumstances, considering what my mother did, you should have told me, Jenny!"

"What difference would it have made? It was done when I saw you."

"You're always so cool and right, aren't you? So

164

correct, so *principled*. You and your mother —between you, do you have even one heart? Or do you both have stones sitting in there?" He jabbed his finger at her.

"Get out of my car. Just get out. Get out, *get out*."

"I'm going!" He pushed open the door and leaped out.

"There she is, Pennoyer herself." Ferd smiled slyly. Jenny had met him, Rhoda, and Nick on the way to school. She wondered how much Ferd knew about her and Rob.

"Jenny will come, too," Rhoda said. "Won't you, Jen?"

"Another party?" she asked. Nick gave her a warm look from under long-lashed eyelids.

"We're all going to the festival at the Greek Orthodox Church. Nick's sister is going to be one of the dancers, and Nick might even play his mandolin if we twist his arm hard enough."

Nick sidestepped around Ferd so that he was next to Jenny. "My musical talents are strictly private."

"Oh, come on, Nick," Rhoda said, "you're good. And I want you to play."

"And what Rhoda wants, Rhoda gets," Nick said amiably.

"Why not?" Rhoda said.

"Will you come?" he asked Jenny as they approached the school.

"When is it going to be?" Rob was sitting on the stone wall, a girl next to him. Suzi? No, another girl.

165

"This coming weekend, a two-day deal. We're all going Saturday afternoon; that'll be the best time."

Rob glanced over, his face stiff. "I'd love to come," Jenny said. "Principled," Rob had said accusingly. "You and your principles." *Okay, Rob, you think I have too many principles? Well, you don't know everything about me, either.* She smiled up at Nick, the smile stretched, became brilliant, glowing, inviting. *Are you watching, Rob? Are you looking?*

Chapter 26

The house was quiet, everyone asleep. Only Jenny sat up studying in her room. Exams were coming. She was accepted into college, so she didn't "need" the marks, but it was important to her pride to do well. She glanced at the clock. Ten-thirty. She might be finished in another hour.

A knock at her door. "Jenny? Jenny, it's me." Mimi looked in. Her face was flushed, her glasses sat low on her nose, and there was a paper carnation stuck behind her ear. "Come on *out*, I have something to tell you! Frankie and I have something to tell you!" Mimi's ordinarily quiet voice was almost rowdy.

"What is it?"

"No, come on!" Mimi beckoned, then grabbed Jenny's hands and pulled her into the living room where, in a moment, her parents appeared with Frankie shepherding them. Her father was in pajamas, her mother tying the belt of her robe. "What is it, what's the matter?" Amelia said. "Shh, you'll wake up Ethel."

"I'm awake," Ethel said from the door of her room. Yawning, she came to lean against Jenny's leg.

"Everybody, sit down," Frankie said. In the center of the room, he and Mimi held hands. "Mimi and I are engaged!"

"Yup!" Mimi shot out her left hand to display a ring on the third finger. She walked around, showing each of them the gold ring with intertwined hearts. "Isn't it beautiful?"

Amelia hugged her, then Jenny kissed her and hugged her, a long back-rubbing hug. "I'm so glad," she said. "I'm so glad for Frankie."

"Hey, be glad for me, too," Mimi said, hugging back, "I love the goof."

"So she caught you, son," Frank said as he shook Frankie's hand.

"No, I caught her!" he said, and Mimi laughed. "And I'm never letting her go," Frankie added, putting his arm through hers.

"This calls for a drink," Jenny's father said. They moved into the dining room where Frank took a bottle of Johnnie Walker and shot glasses from the bottom of the china closet.

"What about me and Jenny?" Ethel asked as her father passed the liquor around.

"Too young to drink, toots."

"Jenny's not so young."

"Not eighteen yet."

"Oh, Frank," Jenny's mother said. "An occasion like this—"

"No, in this house nobody drinks till they're eight-

168

een. Go get a glass of milk, Ethel, and you can toast, too."

"I want a shot toast," Ethel insisted. Everyone laughed. The child's face darkened with humiliation.

"Wait a sec, I have an idea," Jenny said. In the kitchen she poured chocolate milk into two shot glasses and brought them back. "Ethel, we'll just pretend this is dark scotch. Who cares? I don't."

"Okay—to the happiness of Frankie and Mimi," her father said, and they all clinked glasses.

"To us," Frankie said exuberantly.

They drank. "Oh, my, good stuff," Jenny's mother gasped. "When did you decide?" she asked Mimi.

"We've been talking about it for a week—"

"More," Frankie said.

"And tonight we just made up our minds and went out and got the ring."

"How in the world did you do that so fast?"

"I had it all picked out," Frankie said.

"We're going to the Poconos for our honeymoon," Mimi said.

"Are you getting married right away?" Jenny asked.

Mimi smiled sheepishly. "Uh, not really—not for at least a year, but we made all our plans anyway."

"I wanted to get married right away," Frankie said.

"The Poconos—that's where we went for our honeymoon, Frank. Remember?" Jenny's mother had a soft smile on her face. "We're always saying we're going to go back and we never have been back yet. And it's not even that far away."

"Maybe this summer."

"Oh, no, we always say that."

"This time I mean it. I want to take you on a vacation. You need a vacation. Maybe Jenny will watch Ethel, and you and I—"

"Jenny is going to be working."

"Well, she can take a few days off and watch Ethel, and you and I will go away, just the two of us."

"Oh, do it," Mimi said. "You should do it!"

"You haven't heard the other news," Frankie said. "I'm moving to Buffalo."

"Buffalo," his father repeated. "What's in Buffalo?"

"Mimi is going to school there next fall."

"Your job—"

"I'm not quitting, Dad. I'll put in for a transfer, wait for an opening, then move."

"That's right, that's the way to do it," Frank said, giving Mimi an approving look, as if she were responsible for anything Frankie did that made any kind of good sense.

Sipping the last drop of her chocolate milk, Jenny thought that all *their* lives were going on—her father's, her mother's, Frankie's—continuing, expanding, while her life . . . No, it hadn't stopped, but something terrible had happened. It was as if she had been running along a green path, and then, although the path was still there, she had left it. Veered abruptly off, chosen instead to move slowly, painfully, through thickets of stinging brambles. She had left that green path, she had given up Rob for *them*, for her family. And they had been glad, yes, but all the same, had it made any real difference to them? Had it changed any of their lives? Giving up Rob, she had drastically altered—worsened—her own life, while making barely a ripple in theirs.

The next morning, before anyone else was up, Jenny left the house. The sun in the eastern sky looked like a spilled egg. She picked up a trowel and work gloves in the garage and drove across the city to the cemetery where her grandfather and sister were buried.

It was a cool, windy morning. A blackbird screeched from the top of a tree as she got out of the car. Her sister first. She weeded around the rhododendron they had planted. "Gail . . . hello, Gail . . ." She brushed the stone carefully and traced the letters cut into the small, flat piece of granite. *Gail Jill Pennoyer. Beloved daughter and sister. She died too young.*

Two bikers passed, their spokes clicking, heads bent low over the bars. Jenny moved to her grandfather's stone. The little apple tree she'd planted was in tight pink bud. Only four years old, but already taller than she. And again, weeding, brushing the stone. *Carl George Pennoyer. Beloved husband, father, and grandfather.*

"I've been thinking about you, Grandpa." He had been a man of character, of strong beliefs. Whenever life became confusing, too full of doubts and questions, she called on him, invoked his presence: the straight, stern mouth, the harsh voice, the plain words. "What should I do about me and Rob, Grandpa?" If he were here he'd know; he'd tell her. It

171

would be this or that. No waffling. No confusion. Life hadn't seemed puzzling to him.

She straightened up. The breeze had died down. The trees were still. Even the birds had momentarily stopped their racketing. *Jenny, do what's right.* Did she hear his voice, that harsh, loving voice? *Just do what's right.* "Grandpa? . . . What else? *What's right?*" She waited, listening, but only heard the robins resuming their twittering, wind rising in the trees, and a motorbike screaming past.

But she knew.

Rob. I made a mistake.

A terrible mistake.

Chapter 27

As if Jenny needed them, there were suddenly signs everywhere that, in breaking off with Rob, she had been blindly wrong-minded. Her horoscope, for instance, read, "Believe in yourself and the one you love. Step boldly forward and beware of too much thought."

Then Frankie, speaking to her once more with the ease and friendliness of old times (Why? Because she had given up Rob, proving him "right"? Or because he was happy now with the engagement to Mimi?), Frankie told her that, for Mimi, he would have, without a single moment's hesitation, given up job, home, family—anything at all she asked.

He didn't see how it hurt Jenny, how ironic it was that he could say with simple sincerity, "Jenny, when you love someone the way I love Mimi, nothing is more important."

And in English, reviewing for the final the three Shakespeare plays they'd read that term, Mrs. Tedesco asked the class to consider the theme in Romeo and Juliet. "Think of the swift pace of the play, as well as the sun, moon, and time imagery used throughout.

"It suggests, class, that Shakespeare wanted us to reflect on the importance of cherishing those we love. Treasuring each moment given to us. Each moment," she repeated, firmly scratching the word THEME across the blackboard, "is unique in time and will never exist again. Consider, class, the brief span of Romeo and Juliet's love affair. Only four days. And yet think of the extraordinary intensity with which they lived those four days. *Every moment* of those four days. Their love affair was born, came to a blazing climax"—here, there was some giggling, threatening to spoil the intense effect Mrs. Tedesco's words were having on Jenny—"and died. The *people* died. They lived an entire lifetime in four days. Who of us could say the same?"

All this Jenny took in the most personal way, reflecting with a growing misery that Juliet, though only fourteen, had been far tougher, far braver than she. Juliet had had no doubts: she had met Romeo, recognized what he meant to her, loved him generously, and thrown over not only her family for him, but ultimately and without regret, her life.

Miserably dawdling through the day in school, looking for Rob, she advised herself, Just go to him and tell him the truth. Say, *I made a mistake, Rob.* And then what? They had quarreled in the parking lot only three days ago. Would his blue eyes scan her coldly as he said, *You sure did, Jenny, and now it's too late.* But she didn't see him that day.

The next morning, for courage, she braided her hair, one long braid hanging over her shoulder, and put on moccasins and a red leather belt. Today she would find him, she would be brave, at least half as brave as Juliet, and no matter how coldly he looked at her, she would say her piece. All the way to school she rehearsed her speech, walking slowly and alone so she could go over it in her mind.

Rob, I love you. I should never have broken us up. What we had together was too rare, too beautiful, too sweet. I had no right to do that. It was a terrible thing I did. And then, humbly if necessary, she would ask him to forgive and let them pick up where they had left off.

Her stomach knotted as she imagined their meeting. What would he say? How would he act? By turns she was confident and despairing. Swung from the thrilling thought of his face breaking into a joyful smile to the chilling thought of his eyes blank and uninterested.

Second period there was an assembly, and, as she sat down, she saw him across the aisle. She looked at him, couldn't stop looking, as if she were seeing him for the first time, freshly, as she had that morning so many weeks ago when she knew she *had* to know him.

In the half-dim auditorium a movie on skiing was being projected on a screen. Skiing in June? What was going on? Groans pulsed through the room as scenes of snow-covered mountains flashed on the screen and a deep, well-nourished voice said, "We are here in the 'Alps' of the United States." More skiing shots, lean men and women in zingy blue-and-red ski clothes whipping down steep slopes. But Jenny only watched Rob. As yet he hadn't noticed her. She studied his profile. Seen from the side his nose appeared bigger, more solid. He looked older and somber. Had he changed in these past weeks?

She followed Rob out of the auditorium. There were people ahead of her, people between them. She hurried, keeping his blond head in sight. Down the hall, up the stairs, and then, outside the art room she caught up to him. "Rob!" She reached out. He turned and looked at her, directly at her. A smile—something—went across his face; a flash of teeth, a grimace, as if he were about to embrace her ferociously, or bite her, or choke her. And then he walked away.

She stood in the hall, unmoving, as the bell rang and the classrooms gulped in the students. The hall emptied around her. So it was too late. She had made a mistake, yes, but she had hardly known how final. It was finished. All her brave resolutions meant nothing. She had made mischief with her life and couldn't unmake it now.

"Pass?" a teacher said, frowning. Jenny shook her head and gestured up the stairs. "Get a move on, then." Humiliated, sickened, she went up the stairs. Nothing to be done now but accept.

Accept, accept, accept.

176

Accept that she had lost him.

Halfway up the stairs, she paused and looked back, saw that the teacher, Mr. Glendarren, was still watching her suspiciously.

"Well?" he barked.

What a prison this high school was sometimes! She glared at him, then suddenly she called down, "Mr. Glendarren! Mr. Glendarren, how old are you?"

"What?"

"How *old* are you? Are you twenty-eight? Are you thirty? Do you remember being seventeen?"

"*What?*" he said again, his face expressing outrage and confusion. Was this some clever trick to undermine his authority?

"I'm doing an article for the newspaper," Jenny improvised. "It's to be called 'Do You Remember?' That's your question: Do you remember being seventeen? I want to know, Mr. Glendarren. I want to know what it was like for you!" But without waiting for an answer she went up the rest of the stairs two at a time.

Chapter 28

"This is like old times," Jenny said as Rhoda moved around the Rivers' kitchen in slippers and a pair of frilly short pjs.

"Almost," Rhoda agreed. Jenny washed her hands, then sniffed for the telltale smell of fried food. It was Friday night, and she'd driven to Rhoda's house from work. She was sleeping over.

"Except," Jenny said, "in the past, your parents would never have left you alone for the weekend."

"They're not going away after all," Rhoda said. "We had a fight last night; I don't know who they're punishing by staying home, me or themselves."

"You had a fight with your parents? I don't believe it."

Rhoda sat down at the table across from Jenny. "I told them I didn't want to go to college. I want to find a job, get an apartment, live on my own."

Jenny put down the banana she was peeling. "I don't believe this," she said again. She'd always known Rhoda was going to go to college. The question was whether *Jenny* would go, whether her family would have the money. Rhoda's parents had set up a college fund for her on the day she was born.

"I've got to find out what it's like to take care of myself, Jen. I can't go on for another eighteen years letting them do everything for me." Rhoda's voice was thin. "And please don't tell me that college is necessary or that I'm going on a dead-end street. I heard enough of that last night. I know myself, Jenny. College'll be like high school all over again for me. I'll let things happen to me. I won't make them happen."

"What an incredible change. When did you decide?"

"It's been creeping up on me. Yesterday, I just decided."

"You never gave me even a hint."

"Oh, you've been so preoccupied. You've had your own problems on your mind."

"Rhoda, you should have talked to me anyway." Jenny shook her head. "I'm trying to take it in. Are you excited? How do you feel?"

"Terrified," Rhoda said. "But that's only for you. As far as my parents are concerned, I'm a rock of confidence. They think I'm crazy, by the way." She leaned toward Jenny. "What do you think? Do you understand what I'm going to do? You haven't really said yet."

"What difference does it make what I think, Rhoda?"

"It would be nice to know you were on my side!"

"I didn't mean it that way. Of course I'm on your side. You should know that! But the point is, even if I wasn't, you should still do what's right for you. Look, Rhoda"—she leaned toward the other girl—"you can't make decisions about your life based on what's going to make everyone else happy. And that includes your parents. We're too old for that, both of us."

Later they went into Rhoda's room and settled down on the beds. "I always thought you had the most wonderful room in the world," Jenny said. "A room all to yourself. Such richness."

"And I used to envy you sharing a room with your sisters."

"Oh, you never minded being an only."

"But your family always seemed to have so much going on, so many things happening. I thought you guys led a really exciting life. Jen, isn't it hard to believe that in the fall you'll be going one way and I'll be going another? After all these years of always knowing where we each are and what's happening. It's so sad in a way. Don't you wonder if anything will ever be the same?"

Jenny nodded.

"But no matter what happens to us or how far we go away, we'll go on being friends, won't we?"

"We will," Jenny said, half with passionate conviction, half with an equally passionate hope. Wouldn't letting their friendship lapse be as serious a mistake as giving up love? Were there, after all, that many friendships or that many loves in the world?

Chapter 29

In her room, fresh from the shower, Amelia dropped her towel, and, as she reached into her drawer for a nightgown, saw herself in the mirror. In a few more weeks she'd be a grandmother: images of false teeth, or no teeth, of rocking chairs and little old ladies with humped backs and shapeless bodies. Her? She looked hard at herself. Not the body of an eighteen-year-old, but not that bad either. Her legs had gotten a bit skinny and her arms a bit heavy, but she certainly hadn't let herself go to pot. At the thought she drew in her stomach and straightened her spine.

Two months ago she had had her fiftieth birthday. Fifty years. How had she, Amelia Zenner of the flying arms and legs, become fifty years old? Half a century. And she and Frank married for over twenty-five years.

It was Friday night, the market stayed open late, and Frank wouldn't be home until nearly eleven. Amelia put on her gown and got into bed, sighing with subdued pleasure. Climbing into bed with a book on Friday night was something she looked forward to all week. Sunday was Frank's time off, Friday night, hers.

She stretched her legs. Whew, how good that felt. Seemed as if she hadn't stopped moving for days, rushing from one thing to another. Meeting Mimi's parents now that she and Frankie were officially engaged (*she* seemed nice, but him—oh, no, Amelia hadn't liked him), involved with the fair the PTA was holding in Ethel's school, the usual cleaning, cooking, shopping, dentist and doctor appointments. One thing and then another. Busy, busy, she was always busy. Sometimes she felt as if she were running a race with herself—and losing. In the fall, when Ethel went into first grade she'd look for a part-time job. They could use the money—Jenny in college, Vince and Valerie with a new baby, Frankie and Mimi just starting out . . .

She opened her book, something everyone was reading, called *Lovers Leap*. Her bookmark had been made for her by Gail, years ago, when she was a Brownie. A piece of green material clumsily hemmed at either end with the word MOM stitched on it in yellow thread. Awful little thing, really. Gail had never got the hang of sewing; she used to get frustrated just threading a needle.

It was quiet in the house. Frankie was out with Mimi, Jenny at Rhoda's, Ethel asleep.

" 'And what exactly do you expect of me, Charisse?' he said with an arch smile. Charisse raised a finely plucked eyebrow . . .''

Amelia read the sentence three times. The words

182

remained separate and empty on the page. *Relax*, she told herself. *Relax.*

She sat up in bed, listening to the sounds of the house: the hum of the electric clock, floor creaking, refrigerator buzzing, a sudden scurrying and scratching in the wall. *Mice, must remember to buy traps.* And all these small sounds overlaid by a profound silence. The silence of an empty house.

She pushed her reading glasses more firmly on her nose. Empty house? Not yet, not quite yet. True, in the fall, Jenny would go to school and, soon after, Frankie would follow Mimi, but Ethel was still here. Would be here for years. She was only five; would stay home until she was eighteen, surely, unless . . . *No.* Amelia refused the cruel thought. Accidents like that only happened once in a lifetime. No, Ethel would be safe, all her children, her remaining children, would be safe. Had to be.

She began reading again—*"But for you, Nelson, I would be a happy woman!"*—and closed the book at once, remembering now what she had been putting off remembering. Nell Montana.

She had pushed the encounter in the shoe shop out of her mind. She had pushed what Jenny had told her out of her mind.

Mom, I thought you might want to know. Mrs. Montana is in the hospital.

Why would I want to know that, Jenny?

I just thought—

What, Jenny, what? Did you think I'd go visit her? Did you think I'd bring her flowers? Wish her a speedy recovery?

She—she took too many sleeping pills.

Yes, well, she should be more careful. She's a careless woman!

Amelia closed her eyes, remembering how Nell Montana had said to her, *I was a happy person, a person who liked to laugh and then . . .*

For two years Amelia had clung to the picture of a "drunken driver." A criminal person, a woman in a loose robe stained with egg, a cigarette dangling from the corner of her lips; a woman coarse-skinned, crude, and bleary-eyed with drink.

A slow flush rose into Amelia's face. The woman had looked dreadful, yes. Sleeping pills. Liquor. No wonder. Still, Nell Montana had shocked her. Amelia had not expected Gail's killer to look like that: baby blue eyes and a little round mouth like a girl's, yet over all, like a gauze mask, the tense, lined face of a woman in pain.

Was it possible that she, Amelia—*she*—had been the cause of someone else's pain and anguish? Was it possible that this pain had been more than Nell Montana could bear? More than she deserved? How much pain did any human being deserve?

Agitatedly, she pushed back the covers. "Gail is dead," she said aloud. "My daughter is *dead*."

The dead must be buried.

"I can't forget."

Forgiveness is not forgetting. Why do you confuse the two ?

No, she was not to have her quiet night off. Nell Montana was in the room, a presence demanding answers, begging forgiveness.

She went into the kitchen, looked around for a moment, then settled on the refrigerator, opened it, and emptied it of food. Her best thinking had always been done when her hands were occupied. She filled a pail with soapy water and began scrubbing the shelves, the metal grates, the vegetable bins.

For a while she was soothed by the work, scrubbing off the accumulation of bits of food, washing and rinsing, washing and rinsing.

She set the carton of milk in the right-hand corner of the first shelf where it was always kept, carefully filled the egg holder in the door with the fragile white eggs, and rewrapped the cheeses in aluminum foil. *I could do this blindfolded*, she thought. Her mother had done these same things; in California, Valerie might right now be wrapping cheeses in foil, and someday Jenny, too, would scrub a refrigerator, cover leftovers with waxed paper. Women's work. Was there a woman alive who didn't know her refrigerator as well as she knew her own face?

All at once she imagined Nell Montana doing the same thing, cleaning her refrigerator and filling it with food. Amelia dropped a package of carrots and the refrigerator door swung wide. She stood for a moment, her face burning. Then closing the refrigerator and leaving the rest of the food on the counter, she walked through the house to Ethel's room.

The child snored and Amelia shook her toes lightly. In the dim shadows, Gail's bed stood silent and empty. She had kept Gail's part of the room intact, a shrine to her oldest daughter, as if this would keep her alive. But now she saw that it was like a room in a museum, deathly still, lifeless. She might as well have locked a velvet rope around the bed. No one went near it, no one touched anything, no one, perhaps, even saw it anymore. Gail was dead, and it was her memory only that lived.

Amelia lay down on Gail's bed, pulling the pillow over her face. After a while she lay quietly, brushing at the tears. For two years she had refused to acknowledge Nell Montana's humanity. She had wanted only to make this killer, this drunken driver, suffer as she suffered. She had weighed her grief as if on a scale and concluded that no matter what stones, what burdens, what roses and letters and recriminations were dumped on Nell Montana's side of the scale, her pain (whatever she was capable of feeling, if anything, Amelia had said to herself) could never equal Amelia's pain.

She had held on to her grief, trying in this way to hold on to Gail. Nursing the grief. Feeding it. Never letting it go for even a moment, because to let go would be to acknowledge life. To acknowledge that, yes, she lived while her daughter was dead.

She got up and began rapidly stripping the bed: bedspread, blankets, sheets, everything off, everything in a pile on the floor. Tomorrow she would clear it all out, buy a blackboard and a bookcase for Ethel to fill the space. She pulled up the mattress, bent it over on itself, began untacking the pictures from the walls.

She heard Frank's car in the driveway and went into the hall to meet him. He looked weary, the bowtie he wore at work hanging by one string. "Not in bed?" he said.

"Oh, I was restless. I couldn't settle down. I kept thinking about—her. Nell Montana."

"What about her?"

"I thought—you didn't see her the way I did . . ." Amelia pulled her robe tighter around her. "Jenny told me she was in the hospital. Did I tell you?" He shook his head. "She took too many sleeping pills. An accident, I guess. Or do you suppose it was because I—" She broke off, wetting her lips. "She wanted me to say that I forgave her. Did I tell you that?"

He nodded. "Yes."

"Well, I thought—maybe I should call her up and tell her? . . ."

"Do you?" he said. "Do you forgive her?"

"I want to. I think it's time."

"But do you?"

Her eyes filled. "No, I don't. I don't forgive her. Not now. Not yet."

He put his hand around her shoulder, and they went into the house. She had his towel and pajamas ready, and while he showered she made him a sandwich and opened a bottle of Millers which she brought into their room. Their regular Friday night routine.

Chapter 30

The Greek Fair was packed. Hundreds of people were eating, singing, dancing. The blue cupolas of the church were freshly painted, shining like water. Outside, a huge, striped tent housed long trestle tables and a wooden stage. Inside, booths divided by beads and curtains were crammed with authentic Greek goods.

Jenny fingered a beautiful embroidered dress that cost hundreds of dollars. Was Rob here? Why did she even think of him? She mustn't. Still, she looked behind her, to each side, expecting . . . She moved on. A tray of worked silver bracelets, rings, silver snakes meant to clasp the neck or an ankle . . . painted vases . . . embroidered pillows . . .

A waiter flew past holding an enormous blue bowl on upraised hands. "Cucumber salad," he cried. "Cucumber salad!"

A stone vase . . . a painting full of golds and greens and blues . . . beads green as the sea . . . Wouldn't seeing Rob here be a sign? Surely it would mean something? That, despite everything, she should approach him once more?

"Jenny!" Rhoda took her arm. "I've been looking for you everywhere. Isn't it all gorgeous? Nick is going to play his mandolin. We convinced him." She swept Jenny through the crowds, outside, into the tent. Dancers in white pleated skirts and red sashes were leaving the platform to thunderous applause. The long trestle tables were packed with people eating spinach pie and moussaka and drinking orange soda and coffee.

On the platform, Nick sat on a high stool and tuned his mandolin. "This is a Greek love song." He tossed back his hair. "It's a boy talking to the girl he hasn't yet found the nerve to speak to. He says to her, 'Don't you see how much I love you?' " Nick spoke calmly. "The boy says, 'My heart is so full, please listen.' I don't think I'll do it justice but I'll try." He bent over the instrument, hair falling into his face. Jenny was tremulous. Nick's words and the plaintive cry of the music stirred her.

How handsome Nick was, his head inclined over the mandolin, his hands so delicately plucking at the strings. She longed to be in love with him but it was impossible. For one reason only, a reason that was no reason, was only what it was; she was in love with Rob. Gradually, bit by bit, as he went on playing she forgot Nick, barely heard the music and scanned the crowd, looking for a golden head, looking for Rob.

Chapter 31

There was a letter waiting for Jenny sticking out of the wicker mailbox next to the front door. It was unstamped, her name written across the front. "Jenny." Just that. "Jenny." She knew at once, without any doubt, that this was from Rob.

She went into her room, calling to her parents that she was home. Yes, she'd had a good time, she'd see them in the morning. She closed her door.

Three sheets of notepaper. It began as letters usually do.

Dear Jenny,

The other day you came up to me in school, and you said something. I think you said my name, but I'm not entirely sure. The reason I'm not sure is that I hardly heard you, and the reason for that is because when I saw you, just saw you, I became so enraged I couldn't hear anything. All I wanted to do was hurt you the way you have hurt me.

I controlled myself; I walked away, not answering you. But I saw your face. I saw pain. And I was glad.

I walked down the hall, down the stairs, and then – I came back up on the other side near the art room. Do you understand? I came up behind you and I saw you still standing in the same place. And I knew, for sure then, that I'd done what I wanted to do. I had hurt you.

More than if I had actually hit you. I had wounded you! I felt a surge of something: gladness, delight, something very sharp and alive. I went off to my next class, saying to myself that I had won at last! That, after all, you hadn't defeated me. Yes, I felt victorious.

Do you find that strange? Let me tell you this: Ever since that morning you said we were done and handed me back the elephant, I've felt defeated, mad – no, furious. And – I wonder if you can understand – humiliated. Remember the story I told you about that time I was walking down the street and saw this girl I liked, and she laughed? Because my pants were unzipped? That's the way I've felt for weeks now, that you are laughing at me, and yet at the same time I knew I –

Jenny shook her head violently, so agitated she couldn't continue reading. What was the point of torturing herself this way? She tore the letter in half. At once, she put it on her desk, held the two halves together, and went on reading.

. . . laughing at me, and yet at the same time I knew I was being a little crazy, that this was not your character.

Still, I wanted to get back at you! Let's call it revenge. As if we'd been in a war, and I couldn't let you think you had won. Even if you had. Even if I felt defeated.

So I found someone else, a very nice person in every way, a girl who – well, the point is, she's –

Here, Jenny again stopped, unable to go on reading. She didn't want to hear about that other girl! Suzi! Her stomach jolted; she jumped up and went to the window that looked out on the driveway. Next door the blue light from a TV shone through the windows. Jenny gulped in lungfuls of damp night air. On the street, cars whooshed by. She turned and stared at the torn letter on her desk. Why not tear it again, and again, and again? Destroy it!

But after a long time she returned to the desk, sat down, and bent over the letter again.

. . . point is, she's extremely nice, and we

got to be pretty good friends and – well, I kept waiting for something to happen. Do you know what I mean? Basically, for me to stop thinking about you.

I have had all sorts of crazy thoughts: that I would go to your house in the middle of the night and throw rocks at your window. Break the window, smash it to bits! And you would come running out, afraid, startled. Then you'd see me, and I'd just nod curtly and walk away.

I imagined your car going out of control, you there behind the wheel, stiff with terror, and then I – well, what else? – jump in, pull the emergency brake, switch off the ignition. In a word, save you. You'd fall on my neck gratefully, crying, begging me not to leave you. At which point I'd get out of the car and walk away without a backward glance.

I came up with a lot more variations. And none of them satisfied me. None of them made you go away. You didn't leave me alone, and for that I became doubly angry. My God, you, you queen, you cool queen! I saw you in school, I saw you on the street, I saw you in the hospital, and with that other guy, and how I hated you! Your arrogant smile, your high head, your beautiful, wild, slanted eyes!

And then yesterday – at last you gave me what I had been waiting for. Came up to me, said something – my name? And there was pleading in your eyes. And you were asking me something, or about to. I didn't care what you wanted. As far as I was concerned, you were only asking to be shot down, and I obliged. I walked away and left you standing there.

Hurt you. Yes, I hurt you. Don't deny it, Jenny! I hurt you. I hurt you badly. I did what I wanted to do. What do they say? Revenge is sweet? Something like that. I couldn't get that picture of you standing in the empty hall out of my mind. I won, I won!

Now it's Friday night, I've just come home from work, scrubbed the grease out from under my fingernails and had a shower. I went into the kitchen to get something to eat. I poured a glass of milk and (Why? Why then? Because we used to joke about our big attraction being we're both milk drinkers?) – I poured that glass of cold milk and – realized I'd been a crazy man for weeks. And that I had to write you and be honest.

I remember your saying to me once, a long time ago, right in the beginning, "Do you think we can be honest with each other?" And then another time, "You're honest with me, Rob," and you thanked me as if I'd given you something, given you a gift.

So, Jenny, I don't know what this letter means, if it will mean anything or nothing. I see that it may mean totally nothing, yet I'm writing it and I think I'll find the guts to bring it to your house tomorrow.

I'm telling myself I'm doing it for you, Jenny, because of the honest thing, but to be really honest, I guess I'm doing it most for myself. Spilling myself — my guts — to you this way, telling you that I love you and have been sick and crazy since our breakup. Doing it because I want you back so much and I just can't get it through my head that we are really finished.

I don't know if all this makes sense or not. I only know that it's as true as I can make it, and that's all I have to say now, except, I never stopped loving you.

Rob

"Hello?" An answer on the second ring. His mother.

"Mrs. Montana, I'm sorry to call so late. Is Rob there?"

"He works till eleven tonight."

"At the garage?"

"Yes, Slayton's."

"All right, thank you. This is Jenny. Jenny

Pennoyer. I hope . . . I hope you're feeling better."

"I am. Thank you."

There was a moment of awkward silence, then Jenny said good-bye and hung up. Turning away, she saw what she had missed seeing in her rush to get to the phone. Several cardboard boxes overflowing with Gail's things, each box clearly marked FOR RESCUE MISSION. So that, too, was changing.

In her room she braided her hair, put a blue scarf around her neck, and took her car keys. Her parents were lying side-by-side on the couch in the living room, watching TV. "I'm going out for a bit," she said.

"It's awfully late," her mother said.

"I'll be fine."

"Where are you going?" Her father flipped the switch on the blab-off and sat up.

Jenny hesitated, then said. "Over to Slayton's Garage where Rob works."

Her father's face tightened. "Rob? I thought you two—"

"I tried it your way," Jenny said. "I really tried." She knelt down next to her mother. "Mom, I know it's hard for you." She spoke softly. "I know you may never accept Rob, but I have to do this. Can you believe me when I tell you that what I do is not to hurt you? I don't want to hurt you, either one of you. But I don't want to hurt myself, either. Rob is important to me."

Her mother looked away without speaking.

"Mom—" Jenny bit back the cry and went to the door. Would it never be finished?

She was in the hall when her mother called out, "Jenny?"

"Yes, Mom."

"Drive carefully."

She stopped with her hand on the doorknob, then went back into the room. She stood in the doorway. "I'll be careful. See you both later."

"Not too late," her father said. "I don't want you out too late."

"I won't be."

"Do you have money?" her mother asked.

Jenny nodded and patted her pocket. It was the sort of thing they'd said to her and she'd said to them dozens of times before, but somehow, in its very ordinariness, she felt a message. *All right, we don't like what we're doing, but you're still our daughter.*

She parked on the street outside the garage, a broad thoroughfare of businesses and markets, deserted now, only an occasional car passing. Slayton's big lot was nearly empty except for three cars lined up at the back. The gas pumps stood like dark robots. Inside the building, through the glass window, she saw Rob with his feet up on the desk, a telephone at his elbow, behind him a big clock, a Coke machine, and shelves filled with cans of oil. She glanced at the car clock. Seven minutes to eleven.

There was a gladness inside her welling up like water, like a fountain spilling over, but she held it back. Not yet, not yet, impossible to believe yet . . . Wait . . . wait. . . .

She watched him. Waiting. *Don't go in. Not yet.* Had anyone else ever watched him this way? She saw him complete, in every detail. She might be a thief, a robber. She could hold him up. Go in and demand things from him. *Your money or—*no, not his money, only his life. *Your life, please.* A polite thief, asking for no more than what was hers. *Your life, your love. Pass it over!*

At two minutes before eleven he came out in his gray-striped Slayton's Garage coveralls and locked up the gas pumps. He went back inside, opened a tin of some sort, and lathered his arms and hands. Pulled paper towels off a rack and cleaned off the dirty foam. She watched and waited.

He locked the cash register, put the key in his pocket, came outside again. The car windows were open. She didn't call out. She watched him, only watched him.

He went around to the back of the building and in a moment reappeared with a German Shepherd on a chain. He put the dog inside the station, petting it a moment. Leaving a light on, he came out, tested the door to make sure it was locked, and took a last look around. Apparently satisfied, he walked rapidly down the street away from Jenny.

She turned on the ignition, glided slowly up to him, past him, then stopped. She leaned out the window. "Want a ride?" He kept walking. Louder. "Want a ride?"

He turned, looked at her, said nothing.

A terrible thought came to her. The letter—what if the letter had been a hoax? A fraud? His most elaborate scheme yet to get back at her, to take his revenge?

He opened the car door, slid in next to her. And now they looked at each other in the milky light of the streetlamp. *Speak,* she commanded herself. *Tell him about the mistake . . . tell him all the things you were going to say . . . tell him you got the letter . . .*

"Rob," she said.

"Jenny."

And that was all. That was all they said. They opened their arms, went to each other and held. Held each other tightly, more tightly, yet more tightly still, held each other and said nothing. Words were no longer necessary.

About the Author

Norma Fox Mazer's first novel was published eleven years ago. Since then, eight more have appeared, many of which have won awards and citations — the Christopher Award, the Lewis Carroll Shelf Award, *The New York Times* Best Book of the Year, ALA Notable, ALA Best Book for Young Adults. Her novels have also been translated into several languages.

She and her husband, Harry Mazer, also an author published by Scholastic, live in the country, in the Pompey Hills near Syracuse. They have four children, who are now grown, but were in part the inspiration for *When We First Met*. Norma Fox Mazer says that when her children were growing up, and even now, car accidents were one of her "constant fears." She has always been very aware of the issue of drunken driving and has very strong feelings about it.